THE BEAR'S
SECRET BABY

EMERALD CITY SHIFTERS — BOOK THREE

ARIA CHASE

A Headstrong Woman's Plea For Help

When Shayla Dalton's sister turns her back on her newborn baby, Shayla steps in to raise the child as her own. But when little Aislinn comes down with a mysterious illness that no doctor can identify, the fiercely independent Shayla runs out of options. A visit to Bear Island — and the sexy, abrasive man who doesn't even know his child exists — is their only hope.

A Bear Shifter's Battle for Custody

When Kade Lassiter is abandoned by his supposed mate, he swears off women forever. But when his ex's sister — beautiful, headstrong Shayla — shows up with a sick baby girl that she says is his child, he knows he'll do anything in his power to protect Aislinn. And that means keeping her with him on Bear Island, where she belongs — whether Shayla likes it or not.

A Child's Life Hanging In The Balance

Their contentious custody battle is complicated by their undeniable hunger for each other. But when Aislinn's shifter DNA ends up in the wrong hands, Kade and Shayla have a choice to make. Can set their selfish desires aside to come together and fight for Aislinn's rights — and her life? And will Kade be able to accept his feelings for Shayla and give true love another chance?

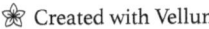 Created with Vellum

STAY IN TOUCH

Sign up for Aria's newsletter to keep up with new paranormal romance and urban fantasy releases, win bookish giveaways, receive opportunities for advance review copies, and more.

"We must take care of our families wherever we find them."

— ELIZABETH GILBERT

1

Shayla shivered faintly as the first sight of the island appeared in the mist the closer the boat drew to it. It looked ominous, though she supposed that was more to do with her own perception based on what Lila had told her, and the boat captain's reaction when she'd asked him to give them a ride to the island. He'd seemed to regard her as crazy and had tried to talk her out of coming there.

The gruff old man came up behind her, as though her thoughts had summoned him. "That's Bear Island," he said in a rough tone.

She nodded. "Yes, I thought it must be, since we're heading right for it." The island was unofficially named Bear Island, according to the captain, though it had no official name. Existing as part of the San Juan Islands chain in the Strait of Juan de Fuca, it was officially uninhabited. Apparently, Kade Lassiter and his people felt otherwise, because they had inhabited it for several generations, at least according to her sister Lila.

"Are you sure about staying, Miss Dalton?" The captain scratched his white beard and sent her a look of disapproval. "Like I said, I won't be back for another month with a delivery of supplies. I can't promise you'll be able to get off the island until then, and the people who live there aren't exactly warm and friendly."

Shayla squared her shoulders and ran a hand down the bundle in the sling. "I'm sure." She wasn't actually sure. She was terrified at the prospect, but she had run out of ideas, and no one else had had the answers as to why her baby niece was not growing despite a healthy start in life.

With a sigh, the captain moved away from her, and they docked at the island less than fifteen minutes later. As the boat's crew, which consisted of three men including the captain, started to unload the supplies, three other inhabitants appeared, seeming to solidify from the mist itself, and their eyes were wide with shock when they saw her step off the boat.

She ignored their response, hesitating for a moment before approaching the youngest-looking one. He might have been in his early twenties. His expression wasn't quite as hard and unwelcoming as the other two flanking him. She forced a small smile, because she couldn't make it any larger with a sudden bout of nerves seizing her, and looked up at him. "Could you please tell me where I could find Kade Lassiter?"

"Who wants to know?" asked one of the men standing behind the younger one, his expression stern, and his voice unfriendly.

"That's personal. If you could just tell me where to find him, I'll get out of your way."

"Outsiders aren't welcome here," said the one who hadn't spoken yet, his unfriendly expression matching the man beside him.

She turned a pleading gaze to the younger man, pinning all her hopes on him. "Please. It's really important."

After a moment, the younger man lifted a hand and waved it vaguely in the direction from which he and the other two had come. "Keep walking straight down the road, until you come to the sheriff's office. That's where you'll find Kade."

She nodded her thanks and hurried away before the other two with him could intercept her, or try to force her back onto the boat. As she hurried through the small village, she was careful to avoid making eye contact with anyone she came across. There weren't many people out on the main street, but she still felt like eyes were on her the entire time as she traversed the length of the town. She shivered as she remembered the conversation she'd had with Lila three days ago.

"You don't want to go to that island for any reason."

Shayla had protested, "It's for Aislinn. Something has to happen. I have to do something, and maybe her father's family knows something we don't. Genetics or something..."

Lila had laughed bitterly. "Genetics. Yeah, that's it. Just stay away from that whole cult."

Shayla had probed before, but her sister had always refused to expound on what she meant by cult when she referred to Kade and his people. At the time, she had issued a small sigh. "Lila, she's your daughter. You can't want her to die."

Lila had sounded cold and utterly convincing when she'd said, "I don't care either way. I would've gotten rid of it if I could have."

Shayla had felt the familiar surge of irritation and bewilderment at her sister's lack of maternal feelings for her daughter, but she had tamped them down. "Fine, if you don't care about Aislinn, then tell me how to get to the island so that I can help her, and do it for me. You still love me, don't you?"

Lila's tone had softened marginally. "Of course I do, even though I don't understand your need to keep that thing. We could have just given it to the foster system, and someone else could have adopted it."

Shayla had persisted, until Lila had finally told her how to find Bear Island.

Now, recalling her sister's words, she wasn't certain if she was allowing them to taint her impression of the town, or if it was simply her own observations and the general air of unwelcome that clung to the place. Whatever it was, she felt like an outsider and vulnerable to attack. It was a ridiculous notion, because people didn't just attack someone for entering their town, but instinct warned her to turn around and run back to the boat.

She might have listened to the fear guiding her if it hadn't been for Aislinn curled against her chest in a warm little bundle. The baby hadn't roused much during the boat ride, or before that. She was so listless and nearly lifeless that it broke Shayla's heart and hardened her resolve to stay. She was probably pinning her hopes on something that wouldn't help either, but she wasn't leaving until she spoke to the child's father and ruled out all possibilities of helping Aislinn.

With her determination renewed, she crossed the last few feet to the sheriff's office before opening the door. As she stepped through the doorway, she took a deep breath for courage and slipped inside the small office.

Small was right. It consisted of one room, with a single jail cell in the corner, currently unoccupied. She was afraid she'd found the sheriff not in, but there was a man seated at the desk in the corner, and he looked up at her as the door closed behind her.

For a moment, she forgot why she was there. His sheer

male perfection stole her breath, and her eyes greedily gobbled up the sight for a moment as she appreciated the wide set of his shoulders, the perfect angles of his face, and the rich brown hair that invited her fingers to run through it. Or might have, if his expression hadn't been so stony. The visible reminder of how unwelcome she was jerked her out of her feminine reverie, and she straightened her shoulders as she walked closer to the desk, not waiting for an invitation.

"Who are you?" he asked gruffly, but his voice was smooth as dark chocolate, with a touch of whiskey.

"My name is Shayla Dalton—"

His nostrils flared, and his unwelcome expression grew darker. "Dalton? As in Lila Dalton?"

She nodded, bracing herself.

"Get out."

Shayla shook her head and planted her feet firmly on the floor as she stood in front of his desk, temporarily eschewing the chair in front of it. "No. I can't do that."

He scowled at her. "If you're here because of Lila, you can just turn around and walk right out again. I haven't seen her in months, and I want nothing more to do with her."

She shrugged. "Lucky for you, Lila feels the same way. I'm not here about Lila though."

His scowl deepened as he leaned back in his chair, crossing his arms over his chest. "What brings you to our island then, Shayla Dalton?"

With a deep breath, Shayla slipped off her jacket, which had been a necessity for the early morning boat ride, even though it was early summer. She laid it on the chair in front of the desk before folding down the corner of the sling so he could see the baby's face. "Your daughter brings me here, Kade Lassiter."

***

Kade was temporarily frozen in shock at the woman's words. He wanted to reject them, but he found himself rising from his desk chair instead and moving around the furniture to get closer to the woman and the baby. "Let me hold her."

The Dalton woman hesitated, clearly torn for a moment before she slipped the baby from the sling carefully, handing over the tiny bundle.

Kade could hold her in one hand, though he used a second one to support her. She was tiny and nearly lifeless, and a dart of concern shot through him. He brought her closer to his face, inhaling her scent from the crown of her head, and his bear rumbled inside him. She was theirs. She smelled like them. This baby was his daughter, and Lila hadn't ever bothered to tell him she was pregnant. His bear roared, and it took all of Kade's control to keep from surrendering to the urge to growl at the other woman standing before him, to direct his sudden rage for Lila toward her instead. "You've brought the baby. Now get off the island before the boat leaves."

Her mouth dropped open, and her green eyes sparkled with dismay that turned to anger. "I'm not a delivery person dropping off your child. I'm in the process of adopting Aislinn, and I'm not going anywhere without her."

"She's mine, and I'll take care of her. You can go now."

The woman, who seemed small to him, though she was above-average height for a human woman, looked like she wanted to stomp her foot at him. She was clearly enraged, and though it should have provoked his temper, it simply brought a surge of amusement instead. He was quick to smother it, along with ignoring his bear's interest in the woman before him. After Lila, he had no intention of getting involved with a woman again.

"I'm not leaving my niece. She's sick, and I'm hoping your people can help her. Lila said you were into...strange things." She looked discomfited as she said the words. "I'm not judging anything. I just hope you can help. The doctors at the Children's Hospital in San Francisco have run out of ideas."

He looked down again at his daughter, already feeling a strong bond forming with her. A surge of anger and dismay shot through him at the idea of the little one not making it. "What's wrong with her?" For one thing, he could guess she wasn't growing properly. She was tiny, and though she couldn't be very old, she should have been larger than she was, especially with her shifter heritage.

"I'm not sure. She was born early, but really healthy. Aislinn weighed almost nine pounds, and she was alert, with good Apgar scores. For the first three or four days, everything was fine, though she lost weight, which is expected. The problem became obvious when she didn't start regaining the weight. At first, she just maintained, but recently, she started to lose ounces that she can't afford to lose. Her main pediatrician has diagnosed her with failure to thrive, and they did a genetic panel to determine if she has a genetic disorder, but everything came back normal."

Kade stiffened slightly at that news, surprised everything had come back normal. There should have been markers or something about her DNA that alerted officials his daughter wasn't quite human. He was relieved they hadn't been able to detect her *ursa sapien* genes, but it was strange. "What have they done for her?"

The Dalton woman reeled off several things, her discouragement obvious as she reached the end of the list.

"Nothing's working. Even the high-calorie formula isn't doing the trick."

Kade nodded, having an inkling of what was wrong, but uncertain. "I want to take her to see my grandmother. Tula raised me, my father, and my six uncles. She might know what to do." He wasn't asking permission, and she seemed to realize that.

She nodded. "We're ready."

He pushed back a surge of irritation, realizing he was stuck with her, at least temporarily. He still had every intention of sending her on her way and keeping Aislinn, but now wasn't the time to argue about that. First, they had to focus on the baby.

2

K ade led her to a small cabin at the end of the street, set a few hundred feet off the main road. She followed behind him, trying not to feel resentful that he hadn't returned Aislinn to her arms. She had to be sensitive and allow him time to adjust to the news that he was a father, and she should be happy that he was interested in the baby and wanted to hold her, but it left her feeling threatened instead.

The adoption was nowhere near final, though Lila had already signed the papers relinquishing her claim. Since Lila had put "unknown" for the father on the birth certificate, it should have been a smooth process, but now she had introduced Kade into the equation. It was the right thing to do, and it always had been, but when she was holding her niece, whom she planned to make her daughter, it was easy to forget the right thing and overlook Lila's lies on the legal forms. Now, she had a feeling it wouldn't be as easy as she had anticipated to adopt her niece.

A surge of dread filled her, sending a pang through her chest as she imagined how it would be to go back to her apartment in San Francisco alone. If Kade decided to keep the baby, he would likely be in a much stronger legal position than she was, since he was the biological father, and he had been denied knowledge of her existence until now.

Realizing she was mentally covering the same ground she had traversed before deciding she had no choice but to bring Aislinn to her father's people, she shoved aside her concern for the time being and focused on Kade and Aislinn as they stepped into the cabin. She closed the door behind them before following him across the main room. The walls were rustic log, and it was on the primitive side, but certainly homey. "Your grandmother lives here?"

He nodded. "With me. And now Aislinn."

She let out a ragged sigh, wanting to snap at him that she hardly needed the reminder that he planned to keep the baby, but decided to let it go. There were more important things to focus on at the moment.

A second later, an older woman shuffled out of the hallway and into the main room. She was tall and solidly built, with a feminized version of Kade's face, framed by steel-gray hair shot through with the occasional silver. She seemed to be stern, but then a gleam appeared in her eyes when she took in Kade holding the baby. "What's all this?" The tone of voice was no-nonsense, but there was nothing unfriendly or cold about her words.

"This is Aislinn," said Kade as he lifted the baby so his grandmother could see her. "She's my daughter."

Tula took the news well, her expression not betraying even a flicker of interest or surprise. "I see. She's a scrawny little thing, isn't she?" It was a rhetorical question, but her gaze homed in on Shayla's, and the first hint of disapproval appeared. "I guess you've been the caretaker, so what have you done to the baby?"

"Grandma," said Kade with a hint of warning. "She hasn't done anything besides bring Aislinn to us when the baby got sick. Be nice."

The old woman harrumphed. "It's hard to be nice when she's clearly related to that Lila woman. They have the same wavy auburn hair and green eyes, although this one's a lot prettier," she added in a slightly grudging manner, though her eyes twinkled.

Shayla started with surprise at that news. She had always considered Lila the pretty one. Her sister was tall and model-thin, and her hair naturally took to pre-Raphaelite type curls. She had a golden complexion, and a natural sexual magnetism that seemed to draw every man in a fifty-mile radius.

Shayla was on the curvy side, a few inches shorter, and she didn't have a golden complexion. Hers was creamy, but she always thought it made her look vaguely vampire-like. Her hair was a wavy, frizzy rat's nest unless she spent hours taming it with styling products and tools, and she usually didn't bother with all that. Clearly, Tula must be sight-impaired.

"The baby isn't gaining weight."

At Kade's words, Tula looked at her. Her expression was neutral, and her voice was politer. "What have you been feeding the poor thing?"

"Formula, since breastmilk wasn't an option." She hadn't even broached the subject of Lila pumping breastmilk for the baby, knowing her sister would have soundly rejected the idea. She wanted to forget Aislinn had ever existed, and she had been eager to sever all ties with the child, so she wouldn't have been open to providing breastmilk for even the first few months.

The old lady made a scoffing sound. "Our kind can't make it on human formula."

Shayla's eyebrows rose of their own accord, and it hovered on the tip of her tongue to ask what the old woman meant, but she held back the words. She told herself it was because she didn't want to distract Tula from focusing on Aislinn, but she also acknowledged that a strong part of it was she didn't even want to know herself.

There was something different about Kade and his people, and she was content not to know what that was, at least for the time being. Whatever it was, it had scarred Lila, making her turn her back on her own child, so Shayla was in no hurry to find out any truths, if they existed.

She followed behind Kade and Tula, having nothing else to do, as they went into the kitchen, and the old woman opened the refrigerator. She watched with interest and a hint of dismay as Tula removed a chunk of salmon and several blueberries from the refrigerator. Her brow quirked as she saw the old woman put it in a food processor, producing a pinkish blue paste within a few minutes. As Tula scraped it into a bowl and selected a tiny teaspoon from a drawer, she realized the old lady planned to feed it to her niece. She opened her mouth to protest. "Aislinn's only seven weeks old. She can't possibly eat that."

Tula waved a hand in her direction, not looking up from the task she was completing. "Your kind couldn't handle it, but ours can."

She could either push for an explanation she didn't want, or she could subside into silence. The idea of feeding a seven-week-old baby salmon and berries didn't sit well with her, but at this point, she supposed it could do no harm. And if it helped, she'd be in line giving daily feedings herself.

Since the pediatrician could offer no hope or solution, what other option was there? She had come here with the intention of finding an answer, and perhaps Tula had it. She had to trust the old woman enough to let her try.

Since they lacked a highchair, and Aislinn couldn't sit up anyway, Shayla watched with amusement as Kade sat at the kitchen table, arranging the baby in his hands, with one hand supporting the back of her neck, and the other keeping her in a semi-upright position. Tula spooned up a bite of the salmon berry paste, bringing it to the baby's lips.

Shayla expected her niece to grimace or try to turn her head, but instead, the baby's nostrils flared, and her mouth opened with more enthusiasm than she had displayed for days. The bite disappeared between her lips, and not a bit dripped out. There was slobber, but no food. Her niece had almost inhaled the salmon paste.

Feeling strangely boneless, Shayla collapsed into the nearest chair and watched the infant devour at least two ounces of the salmon and berries. It was like her niece was starving and had finally been offered real food. Was that what it really was? Had she been slowly starving on the human formula, because something was missing from it? And why was Shayla suddenly calling it human formula too? It wasn't like her niece had been given goat formula or kitten formula. She'd been given human formula, because she was human.

But what if she wasn't *completely* human?

Shayla quickly stifled that thought before it could lead her somewhere she didn't want to go. Instead, she blanked her mind as much as possible and simply enjoyed the sight of Aislinn responding again and starting to move in random ways. Her arms were waving, and there was already more color in her cheeks.

For the first time in more than two weeks, Shayla felt optimistic about her niece's chances. Ever since the doctor had delivered the dour news that he couldn't discover what was wrong with the baby, and nothing seemed to be working to help her, she had been bracing herself for the inevitable moment when Aislinn just slipped away. Now, thanks to the Lassiters, the baby had a chance again.

It filled her heart with warmth, even as the thought nibbled at the back of her mind that she could still lose Aislinn—not to illness, but to the baby's biological father. It was obvious he was already bonding with her, and he would probably be reluctant to let Aislinn go.

She couldn't think about that now. Instead, she just had to focus on the moment and ensuring Aislinn regained her health.

3

Shayla was having a difficult time sleeping, mostly due to the absence of Aislinn, who hadn't been more than a few feet from her since the day she was born. Earlier in the evening, Kade had taken Aislinn with him to his room, giving her no chance to protest.

She guessed she was lucky to be in the same house as her niece, and she doubted she would have been if it hadn't been for Tula's hospitality. The old woman had shown her to a small bedroom at the back of the cabin, and it appeared it had once been a closet converted to a guest space. It was tiny, but it accommodated her needs for the time being. She would have slept leaning against the corner of one of the rough log walls if required in order to stay with Aislinn.

She was awake and alert instantly when she heard footsteps in the hallway. Judging from the impact, it was probably Kade. A quick glance at her watch revealed it was roughly around the time Aislinn would have her two a.m. feeding, though the baby wasn't on a rigid schedule. She could have turned over and tried to go back to sleep, allowing Kade to get the full introduction to parenthood as quickly as possible, and as roughly too, but she missed the baby. That was absolutely the only reason she got out of bed, slipped on her shoes, and padded down the hallway to follow them after opening the door to her room with a tiny squeal of the hinges. It had nothing to do with Kade himself.

She found them in the kitchen, and her lips quirked with amusement as she watched Kade trying to balance Aislinn in one hand while measuring out scoops of formula into a bottle with the other. She'd had lots of practice with the maneuver, but it was still foreign to Kade. She couldn't help a small giggle when he misjudged where to put the scoop, and white powder cascaded down the side of the bottle, leading him to curse.

At the sound of her laughter, he whipped around, scoop and formula in one hand and the baby in the other. He was instantly alert, but it was such an incongruous sight that she couldn't help another giggle. He scowled at her. "I'm happy to be a source of amusement for you."

She forced away any signs of glee as she moved across the kitchen toward them. "Here." Shayla wiggled her fingers. "I can make the bottle."

"I need to learn how to do it," he said gruffly.

She let out a long sigh before holding out her hands. "Fine, then let me take Aislinn while you make the bottle."

With obvious reluctance, he handed over the infant before turning to the task of mixing her formula.

Shayla frowned slightly, surprised that Aislinn felt a little heavier than she had earlier. Could she have already gained weight in the last few hours? It seemed unlikely, but she decided not to question it too closely. It was a good thing if her niece had gained some weight, because the baby desperately needed it.

After moving to the kitchen table and sitting in a chair,

she examined her niece, feeling like she hadn't seen her for days instead of a few hours. She was encouraged to see a bright gleam in Aislinn's eyes, along with more animation in her expression than she had shown for several days. She still had the hollowed-cheek look, but the dark circles under her eyes had faded significantly. Aislinn was clearly thriving here already.

It was bittersweet, because she was thrilled to see the baby on the road to recovery, but also upset because it seemed like her niece didn't need her any longer. She was certain if Kade had his way, she wouldn't be part of Aislinn's life. The thought filled her with dread, and she couldn't help wanting to cry. Tears burned the back of her eyes, and she blinked several times to keep them in as Kade sat at the table beside them.

"Give me my daughter." It wasn't a polite request.

She shivered slightly at the menacing growl in his tone before hugging Aislinn one more time and handing her back to Kade. Tears couldn't be denied any longer, and though she blinked rapidly again, this time they spilled from her eyes.

He made a harsh sound. "Don't try the tear game with me, Shayla. I won't be manipulated by that again."

She ignored him for a moment until she had regained her composure, wiping her face with one of the napkins from the stack in the center of the table. After clearing her throat to enable her to speak clearly, she asked, "What do you mean by that?"

He grimaced. "Your sister is a master manipulator, and anytime things weren't going her way, out came the waterworks. I won't fall for the Dalton-girl trick again."

"That trick always worked on our father, but our mother never really fell for it. I didn't know Lila was still using tears to get her way, but I can assure you mine aren't some way to manipulate you."

"Why are you crying then?"

She shook her head at him, almost disbelieving his lack of sensitivity. "It should be obvious why I'm crying. I miss Aislinn, and I'm afraid you're going to try to cut me completely out of her life."

He busied himself repositioning Aislinn, though the baby obviously didn't need to be shifted. "You have a lot of tears ahead of you if they're genuine, because that's exactly what I plan to do. I'm grateful you brought her here, but you're off this island as soon as I can arrange transportation."

She glared at him, crossing her arms over her bosom. "It's not as simple as that, though you'd like it to be. You aren't listed on the birth certificate, and I'm in the process of adopting her. At the moment, *I* am her foster mother, and you have no legal rights."

She knew immediately it was the wrong thing to say. She could tell by how he seemed to grow larger in the chair that he was enraged. It was an inappropriate moment to notice that even in his anger with her, he was still gentle with Aislinn, ensuring she was comfortable and still drinking her bottle before he leaned forward slightly to glare at her.

"Don't tell me what my rights are when it comes to my daughter. Lila has already screwed me over enough, and so have you. If you want to make this a legal battle, I can do that. There's no need for it though. She's mine, and she stays with me. She'll grow up with her people, not yours."

Things were rapidly escalating, perhaps to a point where nothing could be salvaged. Shayla took several deep breaths in an attempt to calm herself, not speaking again until her own surge of anger had started to fade. "I understand your position, but I'm asking you to understand mine. I love Aislinn. I had intended to adopt her, and I still want to. Please don't cut me out of her life."

His expression didn't soften, though his voice wasn't quite as angry. "You were perfectly willing to cut me out of hers. Obviously, you knew who her father was all the time, but you went along with Lila's lie by not putting my name on the birth certificate. If the baby hadn't gotten sick, you never would have told me about her, so why should I show you any consideration when you didn't show me any?"

It was a good question, and Shayla searched for an answer that would get through to him. Finally, with a sigh, she said, "There's no good reason for you to. I'll concede that, but I'm asking you to consider Aislinn too. She loves me as much as I love her. It's going to be confusing and bewildering for her if the only mother she's ever known is suddenly gone."

"She's young. She'll adjust."

A new wave of tears pressed against the back of her eyelids, and she refused to allow him to see them fall this time. Without another word, Shayla pushed away from her chair and strode from the kitchen, returning to the tiny bedroom at the end of the house, where she took some measure of satisfaction from slamming the door behind her before she allowed the tears to fall.

***

K ade was in the process of burping Aislinn when his grandmother joined him in the kitchen. "I'm sorry we woke you."

She waved a hand to dismiss the notion. "It's fine, but what isn't fine is outright cruelty."

He frowned in confusion. "What are you talking about, Nanna?"

She scowled at him. "You know very well what I'm talking about. You were absolutely brutal with that young woman."

He shrugged his shoulder, refusing to feel any guilt—or at least acknowledge that he felt it. "The sooner she accepts she's no longer needed, the easier it'll be for her."

His grandmother harrumphed. "That's the silliest bit of justification I've ever heard. The truth is, you're angry at Lila, and you're angry at her sister for helping hide the baby from you, so you're lashing out. You're being manipulative yourself, even if you aren't using tears."

He glared at his grandmother, wanting to argue with her, but found he couldn't. "You're right. I'm angry with both the Dalton women. They schemed to keep my daughter from me. Why should I show Shayla any mercy?"

His grandmother's expression softened, and she came to sit beside him at the table. "It's obvious to anyone with eyes that Shayla's a different sort than Lila."

"You have to understand I don't trust my own judgment at the moment. I thought Lila was my mate, and look how that turned out." He barely suppressed a shudder as he remembered the brief, turbulent relationship with Lila. They had met when he was in San Francisco briefly for business, and his bear had prodded him, insisting she was their mate.

The sensation of needing to claim her as his hadn't been as strongly developed as he had expected, judging from hearing others' stories of finding their mates, but it was the first time he'd ever felt such a response, so he had assumed that was the mating instinct coming to life. Until recently, he hadn't understood why his bear had initially thought she was their mate, but it hadn't taken long after he brought her back to the island to realize he and his bear had both been wrong.

Since he'd spoken of forever, and assured her she was the one for him, he'd felt compelled to honor his promises and continue with the relationship. At first, Lila had seemed invested in the relationship too, but then she learned about his shifter abilities, and she had fled. She just hadn't gone alone, and her sister had conspired to help hide his child.

A new surge of anger rushed through him, but Aislinn chose that moment to wrap her hand around his thumb, and a surge of warmth canceled it out. It was difficult, if not impossible, to feel anger or despair while looking down at the infant in his arms. She represented hope and the future, and he knew he was in trouble. This little lady already had him wrapped around her finger, and he'd known her less than a day.

"I'm not saying Lila's sister did the right thing by helping hide Aislinn from you, Kade, but it's obvious the girl loves your daughter. I'm sure Aislinn loves her just as much, and you'll be hurting both if you try to separate them."

He shrugged, letting the topic naturally expire. He wanted to maintain his stubborn stance, but his grandmother's logical words were working insidiously against his angry response. Whether he liked it or not, he was going to have to consider this from a rational perspective and take into consideration what was best for everyone. It was what he naturally did as the leader of their clan, and now he had to do it on a smaller, far more personal scale.

"I'm going to have to do the right thing here, aren't I?" he asked aloud with a resigned sigh a little later.

Tula patted his hand in a sympathetic manner. "I'm afraid so, Kade. You'll survive."

He was certain he'd survive doing the right thing, but would he survive Shayla Dalton being part of his life, even in a peripheral manner? His bear was already clamoring for things Kade refused to consider. He'd sworn to himself that he would remain unmated and focus on taking care of others in the clan. Lila had shown him he couldn't trust his own judgment, at least when it came to women. And there was no denying Shayla Dalton was all woman, and then some.

4

***

Shayla was surprised at breakfast the next morning, which had passed in a mostly silent state, when Kade held out Aislinn to her as he stood up from the table. She took her niece automatically, giving him a questioning look.

"I have to work, so I thought you could watch her while I do so."

The words were gruff, but a concession to the discussion of the night before. She knew his grandmother could have watched Aislinn just as easily as her, so she was touched by his willingness to negotiate and find a place for her in Aislinn's life. She cleared her throat, removing a lump of moisture forming there, and nodded. Assuming a brisk, no-nonsense tone, she said, "Of course. Thank you."

He inclined his head before reaching for his sheriff's hat, which he placed firmly on his head before giving Tula and the baby a word of parting. Shayla tried not to be offended when he didn't include her in it, knowing it was a silly reaction. He had no reason to wish her a good day, or tell her goodbye. She was lucky he was letting her have Aislinn for the day.

She had just finished burping Aislinn when Tula appeared with the mashed-up salmon and berries. It wasn't quite so strange this time seeing the young infant eat the food, but it still felt wrong. She knew it would be one hundred percent the wrong thing to do for a human baby, but there was a niggling suspicion in the back of her mind that Aislinn was more than a human baby. She still wasn't ready to confront that thought, so she shut it down quickly and watched with amusement as Aislinn practically inhaled the food. "She must really like that."

Tula nodded her agreement. "I'm sure she does. The poor thing has probably felt half-starved for the last few weeks."

Shayla nodded her agreement, trying to suppress a wave of guilt. She had done the best she could for Aislinn, even bringing her to this island based more on instinct than any real logic. It wasn't her fault Aislinn's health had deteriorated, but it seemed clear the little girl was going to recover just fine. In fact, she didn't seem quite so little, and Shayla marveled at the thought that Aislinn might have gained a few more ounces from the middle of the night.

In an effort to distract herself from thoughts of how that could be, she seized a random subject and introduced it to the older woman. "What do you do here all day, Tula?"

Tula spent a moment scraping the last of the salmon and berries from the small container before answering. "There's always work to do, of course, and I like to have coffee with my friends. You can take a walk through the forest, or go for a swim in the Strait."

Shayla shivered at the thought. "I never thought to pack

my wetsuit." Fortunately, she had packed a few days of clothing for both herself and the baby, and there should be enough formula to last until the next supply shipment. Shayla didn't know if she would be on the island that long, or if Kade would reverse his position and send her packing far sooner. Either way, at least she was assured her niece had the nutrition she needed until the next supply drop. "I'm not really the nature type."

Tula grinned at her. "If you're going to live here, you'd better get used to it. There's nothing but nature as far as the eye can see. We don't have shopping malls here."

Shayla recognized it as good-natured ribbing, so she didn't get offended. "Do you have stores of any kind?" It was a genuine question, because she hadn't seen signs identifying much of anything as she had walked through the town yesterday.

"Of course. There's the general store, where you go for just about anything. There's also a café if you don't feel like cooking, and there's the post office if you need to mail a package, but you have to understand it won't go out until the next time the ship comes."

"I guess you don't have overnight mail options here then." She strove to match Tula's teasing tone.

Tula shook her head. "There's not much in the way of overnight anything out here, but it's a peaceful way to live, and it appeals to the folks here on the island. Some families have been here for a few generations, while other people are relative newcomers. We're all drawn here for the same reason."

Shayla arched a brow. "What's that?"

"We all want to be left alone," said Tula with a note of seriousness underscoring her words. "We don't want to be immersed in the outside world, so we've created our own little world here."

Shayla gulped. "I see. Did Lila have a hard time integrating?"

Tula snorted. "Lila never even made an attempt to 'integrate,' as you put it. She thought she was queen bee and expected the world to revolve around her." A hint of remorse appeared in the older woman's eyes as she reached across the table to pat Shayla's hand with her own rougher, wrinkled one. "I'm sorry. I spoke more bluntly than I should have."

Shayla shrugged. "Perhaps, but it's nothing if not true. Lila has always been like that, acting as though she's the center of the universe and entitled to anything she wants. Unfortunately, our father was never very good at telling her no, though Mom was far stricter. Lila learned at an early age that if she went behind our mother's back, she could get Daddy to let her do just about anything. She's spoiled and selfish, but I didn't realize just how much until she turned her back on her baby without even a second glance or a moment of hesitation."

"She might have birthed Aislinn, but it's clear to me, even with my old, failing eyes, who that girl's mother really is."

Shayla cleared her throat, unable to speak for a moment as she was overwhelmed once again by the urge to cry. Rather than Bear Island, they should call this place Tears Island, because she'd seemed to be on the verge of them from the moment she had met Kade Lassiter.

She cleared her throat again before speaking. "I do love her. I know it wasn't right to keep Kade off the birth certificate, but I was just so desperate to adopt her before Lila could change her mind. She almost aborted the baby, but when she went in for her appointment, she was farther along than she had estimated. It was too far for her to get an abortion safely, and she couldn't find any doctor who would sign off on giving her a late-term abortion with no good medical reason. And there was no good reason. She just didn't want the baby, but she's the one who must have ignored it for months before finally acknowledging she was pregnant."

Tula let out a soft sigh, one that sounded full of relief. "I'm thankful she ignored it long to take such a course then. Fate has a way of making everything work out."

"I don't believe in fate."

Tula laughed, a sound that was rich with knowledge and amusement. "You will. Just give it time."

Shayla didn't argue, finding no reason to. She couldn't imagine she would ever embrace the concept that there were unseen forces orchestrating her life for her, but she was happy to allow Tula the delusion. The last thing she wanted to do was make an enemy of Kade's grandmother when she feared she was already an enemy of the man himself.

5

A few days later, Shayla knew she could no longer avoid learning the truth. It was simply impossible. After only a few days of the salmon and berries supplementing her formula, Aislinn had grown tremendously. A quick search on Google with her phone had revealed her niece was about the size of the average three-month-old now, and she was holding up her head completely on her own. She was also smiling and starting to babble, which, according to Dr. Google, was unusual at her age.

She was happy to see the changes in Aislinn's state of health, but also certain there was more to it than simple nutrition. With that in mind, she approached Tula that afternoon after Aislinn had gone down for a nap. "I need to ask you something."

Tula stiffened slightly, but she didn't rebuff Shayla as she took a seat at the table. "What do you want to know?" The tone was brusque, much like it had been the first day of her arrival, but there was definitely a hint of warmth underneath it. She had been kind to Shayla from almost the beginning, so she was hopeful the old woman would give her a straight answer.

"Why is Aislinn growing so quickly?"

Tula shrugged her shoulder. "She's just getting the right amount of protein and fat now."

Shayla sighed softly. "Okay, but why does she need a different ratio of protein and fat than a hu...typical child?"

Tula's lips compressed, and she stared at Shayla for a moment. "You'll have to talk to Kade."

A surge of disappointment filled her, though she wasn't entirely surprised to hear the words. She'd hope to have the conversation with Tula instead, because she was more approachable, but she wasn't shocked that the old woman was sending her in Kade's direction. "Do you mind watching Aislinn while I slip out to the sheriff's office?"

Tula shook her head. "I'd be happy to, and she's asleep anyway. The little thing is no trouble at all." When she called Aislinn *thing*, it was with a strong note of affection versus the dismissive and disdainful way Lila had spoken the words.

Feeling reluctant, she got up from the kitchen table and left the cabin for the first time in a few days. After her cold reception at arrival, she'd been hesitant to face the towns-people, assuming they would still be cold and standoffish. Not that she could completely base the attitude of the entire town on the three men she had run into at the dock, along with Kade's less-than-friendly reception. She just inferred the attitude was pervasive.

As she walked to the sheriff's office, she looked around for other residents, but ran into no one. That seemed strange for a lovely summer day, so she figured they must be doing their best to avoid her. She tried not to let it hurt, because what did it matter? The opinion of the people on this island meant nothing to her, and by the time she was back home, she'd forget all about them.

It still upset her to be disliked just because she was an outsider, before they even got a chance to know her.

It was a short walk to Kade's office, and she opened the door without knocking, since it was the Sheriff's Station. Kade was the only one in attendance, just like the last time she had been there, and he looked up from his pile of paperwork when the bell on the door chimed.

She couldn't help teasing him. "This was exactly what you were doing last time. I'm beginning to think you're a paper-pusher, Kade." She hoped she hadn't gone too far when she realized how offensive the words sounded, though she'd only meant them in a teasing way.

Fortunately, his posture remained relaxed, which was a good sign. He had been less stiff with her over the last few days, and he had stopped with his veiled threats that he was going to send her on the next ferry home.

"Being the sheriff on an island with a population of fewer than five hundred is not an exciting whirlwind. It's mostly paperwork. I don't mind it, though. I'd much rather everyone be peaceful and get along."

She nodded as she approached his desk, since he hadn't tossed her out of the office. "I really didn't mean that in an offensive way."

He arched his brow. "I'm aware of that. What brings you by?" He sounded a bit resigned when he asked the question, as though bracing himself for something awful he'd been expecting.

"Your grandmother sent me to you."

"Does she need something?"

Shayla shook her head. "No, but I do. I need some answers."

His expression closed slightly, but he didn't tell her to get out. "Ask your questions then." As he said the words, he crossed his arms over his chest, and his body language radiated reluctance.

"Why is Aislinn growing so quickly? Why did she need different food from a typical infant? And why does my sister insist you're all part of a cult and call you the bear people?" The words tumbled out one after another, until she was practically tripping on them. She hadn't realized how long she'd been stewing over the topic, and the words spewed from her.

Kade let out a long sigh before dropping his arms from his chest and leaning back in his chair. It was as though he'd made a conscious effort to be open to her. "We're bear-shifters."

Her mouth dropped open, and she stared at him in disbelief. Part of her had been gearing up for some kind of strange revelation like that, but she wasn't really ready to embrace the unknown just yet. She shook her head. "You mean you think you're bear-shifters?"

His eyes flashed with irritation. "No, I mean we can shift into our bear form at will. Would you like to see?" His tone of voice indicated he wasn't actually receptive to showing her.

She wasn't ready to see it anyway. She shook her head emphatically. "How does one become a bear-shifter?" It was an insane question to ask, but it fit right in with the conversation and how she was currently feeling—completely nuts.

"One is born a bear-shifter," he said in a slightly biting tone. "It's not like a magical spell or anything that gets cast on you. *Ursa sapiens* simply took a different evolutionary path from *homo sapiens*. That's all there is to it."

She nodded, though she was still struggling to absorb his

words. He made it all sound so simple, but it was anything except easy and uncomplicated. Either they were all crazy, or they were all bear-shifters. The rapid changes she had seen in Aislinn, which were outside the norm even for a baby playing catch-up on her growth, lent credence to his assertion that they were bear-shifters. Abruptly, she remembered Aislinn had been born with a thick covering of extra hair that had fallen out within two or three days after birth. It was another anomaly, and another point to support what he was saying.

"Did Lila know?"

He grimaced at the sound of Lila's name. "Not to start with. We don't go around revealing our heritage to everyone we meet."

"You brought her to your island, and she didn't know what she was getting into?" It was difficult to hide her disapproval, and she was slightly sympathetic to the decisions Lila had subsequently made—though not sympathetic enough to understand how Lila could be so callous to her own daughter though. "When did Lila find out?"

"First, you have to understand Lila wasn't happy here on the island. It only took a few days for her to grow bored with our simple way of life, and she started pestering me about adding the island onto the ferry routes and finding ways to expand our contact with the outside world. She didn't respond to my gentle suggestion that she should learn to adapt, so I firmly told her there would be no changing our way of life. At that point, I hoped she would leave, but she didn't. She decided to stick it out, I guess."

Shayla's eyes widened. "Why did you hope she would leave? You're the one who told her you wanted to marry her. She called and told me that before she ever ran off to live on the island with you." At the time, she had considered her sister impulsive and on the crazy side for running off to elope with a man she barely knew. There'd also been a strong element of envy to her response, because she'd wished she had felt something strong enough for a man to be willing to risk everything to be with him.

Kade's mouth tightened, and he ran a hand through his brown hair as though searching for the words for a moment. Finally, he nodded. "I did say that, and I meant it at the time, but I soon realized I had been mistaken. Your sister wasn't who I thought she was."

She arched brow, feeling defensive on Lila's behalf. "Clearly, you weren't what she thought you were either. If you'd both tried a little honesty..."

He glared at her. "I wasn't going to bite her until she knew exactly what we were. When I first met Lila, my bear whispered that she was ours. I never had that reaction to a woman before, so I assumed it was the mating instinct flaring to life. I'd heard it was all-consuming and intensely passionate, but this was more of a quiet whisper in the back of my head. I figured I just didn't have as strong a reaction, or perhaps other bear-shifters had exaggerated the pull of meeting your mate. It was a whirlwind relationship, and I already had her back on the island before I realized my bear had been mistaken. She wasn't our mate. I know now why we thought she was, but she wasn't."

It was strange and slightly upsetting to hear him refer to himself in the third person as we versus he, and his words were also disconcerting. "If you really are a bear-shifter, how can you make such a mistake?"

His shoulders stiffened, and he seemed to be bracing himself for something. "It happens occasionally that our bears get confused, especially if there's a close link between our mate and someone else. It's usually a biological link, and they share a similar scent."

She shook her head, unable to grasp his words. She understood the individual definition of each, but put together, it was a perplexing sentence. "What do you mean?"

"To be blunt, my bear mistook Lila for our mate because her scent was similar to her sister's. My bear insists you're our mate, and Lila never was."

6

In a panic, Shayla reared back from the desk, eyes wide as she searched for an escape route.

Kade let out a ragged sigh. "Relax. I'm not going to pounce on you. I have no intention of acknowledging or acting on my bear's insistence. After the last disaster, I've sworn off relationships, especially with Dalton women. You're perfectly safe."

Why did his words fill her with disappointment rather than relief? She sagged slightly, taking a deep breath. "Thank you for being so honest with me. I'm still not sure I believe everything you've said, but I'm trying to keep an open mind."

He shrugged his shoulders. "How open you are is up to you completely. For my part, I'm still perfectly happy to send you back on the next ferry, but it's clear Aislinn is attached to you. If you can blend in with our way of life, you can stay. We'll find you a little cottage or something, or build you one. You should know, though, that Aislinn stays with me."

She swallowed the sudden lump in her throat and nodded. "Yeah, okay." She couldn't really argue with him, and not just because he could supposedly shift into an eight hundred-pound bear. He was Aislinn's father, and he understood the challenges ahead of his little girl far better than Shayla ever could. That he was willing to allow her to stay on the island and be part of Aislinn's life was more than she had expected. She wasn't exactly at the point of gratitude, and was still feeling more resentful than anything that he had co-opted the baby so efficiently, but she could appreciate the gesture and respond kindly. "Thank you. I have no intention of leaving Aislinn."

He nodded, apparently satisfied. "We'll figure out living arrangements soon then. If you'll excuse me, I need to get back to work."

She tried to tell herself she wasn't feeling hurt at his abrupt dismissal, and she turned on her heel and strode from the office. Her mind was awhirl at what she'd just learned, and she wondered how she would ever process and accept it all.

***

The words on the papers before him blurred into an illegible mess, and Kade realized he was squeezing the pen tightly enough to break it, a millisecond before the plastic yielded, spilling ink all over his hand and the paper, along with embedding a shard of plastic into his finger. With a small curse, he reached out and tossed it in the trash before reaching for a tissue to dab at the small cut. It healed almost instantly, thanks to his shifter genes, and he quickly forgot all about it.

He was too busy thinking about Shayla, and the way she

had reacted first to the news that he was a bear-shifter, and secondly that she was his mate, at least according to his bear. He hadn't lied to her when he said he no longer trusted his bear's instincts, at least when it came to mating. He also hadn't been completely truthful with her. When his bear had mistakenly thought Lila was their mate, it had been a tepid response, not the consuming, compulsive need to claim her as theirs. The more time he spent with Shayla, the clearer that urge became, and the harder it was to resist it.

He truly had no intention of having another relationship and had decided to remain single even before Aislinn came into his life, with her luscious and curvy aunt along as part of the package. Unfortunately, his bear wasn't on board with that idea, and it was an internal struggle to keep the animal in check whenever he was around Shayla. His body and his mind were at war with each other, and it was a state that couldn't persist. One of them had to win and quickly, but he wasn't confident enough to place bets on whether it would be his human brain or his bear instinct that finally triumphed.

It had been wise not to share that with her, or she would have run screaming from the office. She hadn't even seen him shift yet, and she was already terrified of the idea. That should have helped his human side conquer the ursine side, but it simply made his bear insist more urgently in his head that they had to claim her before she could leave them. That wasn't Kade's style, and he forcefully roared back at the bear to shut up and let him work.

For a change, his bear side calmed down and listened to him, though he felt it sulk even as he immersed himself in paperwork that still remained a blur.

7

I t had become Shayla's habit to get up in the middle of the night when she heard Kade and Aislinn stirring in the kitchen for the baby's feeding. For a moment, she was tempted to cower in her room and avoid him entirely, but that would do nothing to acclimate her to the differences between herself and the bear-shifters. If she was going to live on the island to be near Aislinn, she couldn't hide for the next eighteen years in this tiny guest room, or whatever cabin eventually became hers.

Squaring her shoulders and sighing in resolve, she reminded herself he wasn't going to eat her. Probably. She slipped on her robe and slippers before walking out of the room and finding them in the kitchen.

Kade had gotten more adept with bottle preparation, and by the time she joined them at the table, he was already holding a full bottle for Aislinn, who was sucking it down greedily and with an occasional murmur that sounded like approval. She took the seat beside them, watching Kade's large hands as he tenderly cradled the baby and held the bottle.

He was clearly strong, and if he could change into a bear, his strength was beyond what she could ever imagine. He was gentle too, and it was obvious in each touch and word directed at his daughter. The juxtaposition of strength and gentleness moved her on a feminine level, but not one that was purely maternal. She enjoyed watching him take care of the baby, but it wasn't strictly because she knew he was caring for Aislinn.

She blinked when she realized she was imagining his large hands moving with that same care and dedication over her soft curves. Shayla cleared her throat, searching for something to say, but drew a blank. Finally, she said, "You're really good with her."

He looked up, seemingly startled at her words, though his expression softened. "She's mine. I take care of what's mine." His words were protective, but also slightly ominous. Or perhaps too strong, with a hint of warning.

But what was he warning her about? Was he telling her he would protect Aislinn from everything, including Shayla? Or was he giving her a warning that once he claimed something as his, he took care of it? The idea of being claimed by Kade should have been abhorrent, but instead, it sent a surge of warmth through her, and her nipples tightened against her pajama shirt. She was glad to have the thick terrycloth robe hiding proof of her sudden arousal.

"You never questioned that she was yours. I expected you to want a DNA test."

He shook his head. "I knew she was mine as soon as I held her. She has my scent."

She nodded, reluctantly fascinated, though it meant accepting what he was saying as the truth. "How does that work for you? Do you see something when you...scent?"

He shook his head. "It's more of just an instinctive understanding about things. It's difficult to explain if you don't have the shifter instinct, but it's...I suppose like really strong intuition. You quickly learn not to ignore your bear instincts, because they're usually spot-on."

She bit her lip, debating about whether to call him on that, since he had said earlier today that he had no intention of acknowledging his bear's insistence that she was their mate. Finally, feeling cowardly, she let it go for the moment. "Does Aislinn have that already?"

He shrugged. "She probably has a keen sense of instinct, but it's not fully developed yet. She'll gain the ability to shift at puberty, and with it will come a more defined sense of her bear and instinct. If she's in danger before then, or extremely emotional, it's likely she'll be able to connect with her bear side, but it won't be a common occurrence for her until puberty."

"Isn't it strange sharing your head with another presence?"

Kade let out a laugh. "It's not quite like that. I don't hear voices exactly. It's just a sense of what my bear wants. Usually, we're in agreement, and it only becomes like a screaming pulse in my head when we are at odds with each other." He held up a hand. "I know how that sounds, but it's not as crazy as I imply. It's kind of like being torn between logic and emotion. Like I said, it's difficult to explain, but there's usually only strife when the human side doesn't want to follow a course the bear side thinks is correct."

"Like claiming me as your mate?" She was surprised at the words, having decided not to face that topic of conversation in the near future, if ever. Yet the words had slipped out without her permission. "You don't have to answer that. I shouldn't have said anything."

His tone was gruff, and his eyes had darkened. "My bear doesn't care about logic and reason, or all the reasons why a relationship between us would never work. He just smells your scent and knows you belong to him. The human side of me knows it too, but I'm not going to surrender to my animal instincts, especially not with this."

She blinked, disconcerted by the burning sensation behind her eyes. "Is there something wrong with me?" She barely bit back a snort as she asked the question. Of *course* there was something wrong with her.

Besides being *just* a human, she was on the average side, with generous curves, and she was certainly not what a man like Kade would be used to. He was a perfect physical specimen and could have any woman he wanted. He'd easily attracted Lila's attention, and her sister was usually selective about her partners, only gravitating toward those who were rich and could take care of her. That Kade could convince her to come to his island and live a completely different lifestyle was testament to how compelling he could be.

He let out a small growl, and it sounded more animalistic than human. "There's nothing wrong with you. I just can't trust my own judgment, and it's far too complicated to get involved with Lila's sister."

She winced at the words. "Yes, because that's all I am. I'm just Lila's sister." With that biting response, she pushed away from the table and hurried back to her room, closing the door and leaning against it as she successfully conquered the urge to cry. He was a jackass, and he didn't deserve her tears. So why was she still yearning for him after his rejection?

She slipped off the robe and forced herself back into bed, but she didn't actually think she'd get any sleep. She was still wide awake with her door opened a half-hour later, the hinges squeaking as they did every time the door opened or closed. She stiffened, but didn't turn to look. There was no need, because he circled around the bed and came to stand in front of her, and she couldn't force her eyes to remain closed.

They popped open of their own accord as he knelt down beside her, his knees probably pressing into the floor to get to her height. He wasn't on the bed with her, and he wasn't touching her, but her skin was suddenly alive, and she felt like there was an electrical current flowing between them. "What are you doing in here?" She tried to make the question sound angry and unwelcoming, but it came out more like a timid shiver.

"I think I hurt you, and I didn't mean to. You're far more than Lila's sister. You're the best parts of what she could have been, but she'll never let herself be so genuine. If you had any idea how difficult it is for me to resist what my bear wants, you'd know how much I want you."

His words cheered her considerably. "It's a terrible idea, isn't it?"

He nodded, even as he lifted a finger to smooth a strand of auburn hair off her cheek. "The absolute worst, and that's comparing all the other bad things I've done in my life, including bringing Lila to the island and accidentally getting her pregnant before she ran away."

"Remind me again why it's such a bad idea?" She wet her lips with her tongue after asking the question, holding her breath as she awaited the answer.

He groaned low in his throat, his eyes following her tongue with evident need. "If I had some perspective and time, I'm sure I could come up with a long list of reasons."

"Yes, me too." She held her breath as his head lowered, his mouth getting ever nearer. She knew she should roll away, or just ask him to leave. She was certain he would do so, and without complaint. He was never going to force her to do anything she didn't want to. The problem was, she wanted to do it, and very much so.

"You should go to sleep now."

She smiled at him. "I can't with you in my room." She tilted her head slightly on the pillow, making it easier for his mouth to align with hers. "Maybe you should kiss me goodnight?"

He groaned again, but he didn't seem to be fighting it any longer. His lips touched hers, first in a gentle kiss that soon grew more frantic. His tongue slipped into her mouth, and she caressed it with her own. Only their mouths were touching, aside from the hand he had buried in her hair, but it felt intimate, as though they were already joined. It was the most intense kiss of her life, and she could only imagine how much more intense making love with Kade could be. Excitement filled her at the thought, and she knew she was ready to embrace Kade, though she wasn't entirely certain about the bear-shifter side.

That was what gave her the strength to pull away. She wasn't sure about the bear in the man, and it wouldn't be fair to him to imply that she was or had already decided she was fine with everything. Until she knew for sure how she felt, she couldn't lead him on. Her body burned for him, and she knew she was perilously close to losing her heart to Kade, but the bear-shifter inside him still frightened her. She licked her lips when she looked into his eyes. "May I see your bear?"

For a moment, Kade seemed unsettled by the request, but then his expression cleared. "If that's what you want. I have to get undressed though. I've ruined too many clothes during shifting."

She managed a shaky smile. "That's the best excuse to take off your clothes that I've ever heard."

Kade grinned at her as he stood up, stripping off the t-shirt and pajama pants he'd worn. He wore no underwear underneath, and her cheeks flushed when she got her first look at his generous manhood. It was a daunting sight, and she quickly ripped her gaze away. She was intrigued, but also slightly alarmed, by the sheer size of him. Waving a hand in the vague direction of his cock, she asked, "Is that a common gift among shifters?"

He gave her a cocky grin. "Yes, but I'm more blessed than many."

She gave him a doubtful look. "How would you know that?"

Clearly unabashed, Kade said, "I've been naked around all of the clan as we shifted. It's just like a bunch of boys in the locker room comparing...notes."

She rolled her eyes, refusing to reveal her amusement at his claims. A moment later, her laughter fled in the face of wonder as Kade crouched on all fours, and a bear appeared where the man had been. It wasn't an instant process, but it happened so rapidly that she had difficulty following the transformation. She caught a glimpse of his nose stretching, and his face reforming into a muzzle, but then it was a bear's face before she could truly focus on how it had become so.

She stared at the impressive bear before her, his fur the same rich brown as Kade's hair. She lifted a hand to touch it, but then hesitated. She was torn between fear and curiosity.

A moment later, Kade bumped her hand with his head, forcing her to touch his silky fur. It was much softer than she had anticipated, and she couldn't resist the urge to stroke it lightly.

She watched his face as she did so, and his eyes seemed

to gleam with pleasure as his lids dropped half-mast, and a rumbling sound issued from him. It sounded eerily like the purr of a cat, and as she moved her hand to rub behind his ear, the rumbling grew louder, and he pressed his furry body more firmly against her. He was clearly enjoying the attention, and for a moment, he was so much like a big puppy that she couldn't help giggling.

Kade's eyes opened with surprise, and a moment later, the man had returned. "What's so funny?"

She shook her head, waiting until her urge to giggle had passed before she spoke. "You're just so sweet and adorable. It wasn't at all what I was expecting."

He quirked a brow. "What were you expecting?"

She shrugged. "I don't know. I guess sharp teeth, long claws, and perhaps some slobbering."

Kade's chest puffed out. "I'll have you know I never slobber, woman."

She giggled again, unable to fight back the giddiness sweeping through her. There was still fear and uncertainty, but it was more closely related now to the other bears in his clan, and how she could fit into their life here. She was no longer afraid of Kade in any form, man or bear. She started to tell him that, but with perfect timing, Aislinn began to cry. She grinned at him. "I guess you're being summoned."

With what looked like irritation, though his gleaming eyes revealed he didn't really mind, he shrugged on his t-shirt and slipped on the pajama pants again. "I guess I'll go take care the baby while you laze around in bed."

She stretched, letting the sheet fall enough to reveal her cleavage in her tank top. "I guess so. I'm going to go to sleep now. I bet you'll have a long night."

He glared at her. "I have a feeling you're going to have a long night, too, because I can smell just how aroused you are. There's going to be intense suffering for both of us tonight."

She was startled by his words, and her cheeks flushed, but she didn't try to deny them. What was the point? If his smelling was that acute, he could definitely tell how much she wanted him, and she was sick of lies and deception anyway. "Maybe we'll get another chance soon."

His eyes darkened, and his desire was obvious. "Very soon." He almost growled the words, but they were like a promise he was making, and she gladly embraced it.

8

S urprisingly, after Kade's departure, Shayla had slept like a baby. She woke refreshed and had just slipped on her robe when there was a pounding at the front door. She slipped out of the room and ran into Kade and Aislinn in the hallway. A spark of sympathy shot through her when she saw the bags under Kade's eyes and his hair standing on end. It looked like he'd had a rough night, and she wasn't certain if that was because Aislinn had woken more than usual, or because he'd been left in a state of frustration that had him tossing and turning.

The person at the front door pounded again, and Kade scowled in clear annoyance. "Someone had better be dying, or they will be," he said gruffly as he strode ahead of Shayla to open the door.

She walked with him, but stood back, certain it would be something to do with the clan's business, which meant it wasn't hers. She stiffened when she heard her name and stepped into view, frowning at the tall, almost gawky, man standing at the door. He wore an ill-fitting suit, and his hair was windblown, indicating he had probably arrived by boat.

"Who brought you here?" asked Kade, his voice thick with suspicion.

"I hired a fisherman at the pier in Seattle. That hardly matters, does it? Now show me to Shayla Dalton."

Shayla cleared her throat. "I'm Shayla."

The dark-haired man examined her for a quick moment before nodding, apparently either recognizing her or accepting her word. "I'm Jeffrey Brogan with Child Protective Services." He pulled out a bifold leather wallet and opened it to show his identification before rapidly flicking it closed and sliding it back into his pocket. "I'm here regarding Aislinn Dalton."

There was a definite growl in Kade's tone as his arm tightened around Aislinn. "What about her?"

"The infant is seriously ill and should be in a hospital. I've come to take custody of her and see that it's done."

Shayla swayed under the shock of the news, already shaking her head. "Her pediatrician never said that. He told me he had to make the official recommendation that she stay in the hospital, but if it were his daughter, he would take her home and love her until she passed away."

The CPS agent scoffed, as though he knew more than the physician. "We don't agree with that recommendation at all. If the child is still alive, she needs to be in a hospital."

"My daughter is perfectly healthy," said Kade.

Brogan frowned at him. "Just who are you?"

"I'm Sheriff Kade Lassiter, and Aislinn is my daughter."

The other man paled slightly and looked down at his phone, as though reading an electronic file. "I see no mention of a father here."

"That was because my sister was being dishonest so she could push through the adoption. Kade is definitely Aislinn's father."

"Well, of course we will have to prove that through DNA, but it hardly matters at the moment. He's clearly busy with his own child, and I need the infant."

Shayla shared a puzzled look with Kade. "What are you talking about? Aislinn's right there." She pointed to her niece on Kade's shoulder.

The CPS agent shook his head, his expression full of disbelief. "That's impossible. She was diagnosed with failure to thrive and on the brink of death. That couldn't possibly be the same child. She's far larger than I expected."

"She got better," said Kade. "As you can see, there's no need for your concern, so you can start swimming back to Seattle."

Brogan glared at him. "I'm not going anywhere without the infant in question. That can't be Aislinn Dalton."

"It is. Why don't you compare her DNA to the samples you have on file? I know the state ordered genetic testing at the pediatrician's behest when Aislinn wasn't growing." Since Aislinn hadn't officially been adopted as hers, she was still on the state health insurance plan, so they had been the ones to pay for her genetic testing.

The CPS agent looked surprised for a moment, and his mouth gaped open and closed before dropping open again. He seemed to be on the verge of arguing, but clearly couldn't find a reason to do so. "Very well. I'll collect a sample of DNA. When we get back to the city, I'll compare it, and if it's a match, I'll let you know. At that time, you can visit the child."

Kade shoulders stiffened, and his stance widened. "What you'll do is conduct your DNA tests here by bringing in whatever expert you need, and Aislinn will stay here until you verify it's her, and she's in fine health. At that point, CPS will bow out."

The CPS agent glared at him. "I'd like to know what you think you're going to do about anything, especially telling us what we're going to do. A rural sheriff is no match for the California DCFS."

"For one thing, I'm going to call my good friend Kingston Meade, and he'll send the best attorney available for custody disputes. I'll also have that attorney file an immediate injunction preventing you from removing Aislinn before you verify her identity, and further, we'll get a protection order against you personally."

The agent sputtered, though his posture shrank inward. "I hardly feel all that's necessary."

"To be blunt, I don't care what you feel. I'm protecting my daughter."

Brogan sighed. "Let's compromise. I'll take the sample and send it off, and then I'll stay here on the island until it's cleared. Once we prove or disprove the child's identity, or find the real Aislinn, then events can move forward."

Shayla didn't like his vague wording, and she was inclined to send him packing, but she wasn't entirely certain Kade could do all the things he had listed, at least not in a short timeframe. "Wait, you're going to do the DNA test?"

He gave her a look full of exasperation. "Isn't that what we've been discussing?"

She glared at his tone. "I meant you personally. Are you qualified to do that?"

He sniffed at her. "I carry a kit with me, though of course I can't do the diagnostic testing here...I mean myself. There's no reason I can't collect the sample from a swab of her cheek and send it off though."

"We'll have the attorney drop it off in Seattle on his way back." Kade made the offer, though his gaze was cold.

Brogan shook his head. "I already said an attorney isn't necessary."

Arching a brow, Kade asked in a dangerously soft voice, "Are you trying to advise me that I don't require an attorney? Doesn't that seem contrary to your training?"

Brogan stiffened. "You must do as you wish. If it's someone I can trust, I'll entrust the sample to him."

Kade inclined his head, though he was still visibly angry. He turned to Shayla, holding out Aislinn. "Watch her while I get this person settled somewhere."

"There's an empty jail cell," she said under her breath, eliciting a small smile from him. As soon as Aislinn was in her arms, she hugged her niece tightly as fear of being parted from her swept through her. This was the second time in recent memory she'd faced losing the infant, and this time, she knew Aislinn wouldn't be going to someone who loved and protected her.

She didn't trust the CPS agent. Perhaps it was simply because he wanted to remove the child from them, but she already disliked him heartily. He might just be doing his job, but she hated him and everything about him.

Kade didn't bother to change out of his pajama pants and t-shirt, though he did push his feet into boots as he directed Brogan away from their cabin, and she closed the door behind them. After the wooden barrier was between them, she relaxed slightly, feeling safer, even if it was an illusion. Aislinn cooed at her, and she turned her head to nuzzle her cheek against the baby's. "Don't worry, sweetie. You aren't going anywhere." The words were as much for Shayla's benefit as Aislinn's.

***

S hayla discovered that afternoon that Kade hadn't been bluffing. When he came by the cabin and asked her to bring the baby to the sheriff's office, she immediately complied, following behind him. When she entered the small building a couple of minutes later, her eyes immediately registered Brogan, but there was also another person standing there. In her crisp corporate suit, no-nonsense black heels, and clutching a briefcase that probably cost more than Shayla's last car, the Asian woman was as out of place on the island as the CPS agent. She wore a warm smile, and she was standing far enough apart from Brogan to indicate she wasn't aligned with him. Shayla wasn't certain if it was a conscious decision or an unconscious response to Brogan himself. Either way, she guessed and correctly that this was Kade's attorney. He confirmed it a moment later with introductions.

"Shayla, this is Tru Song, and she'll be protecting Aislinn's best interests."

As she held out her hand to give Shayla's a firm shake, the attorney added with a sparkle in her eyes, "Which means I'll be insuring she stays with you folks."

Brogan let out a sound that indicated he was annoyed, but he didn't offer any words to the contrary.

"It's nice to meet you. It's also nice to know someone's looking out for Aislinn besides us."

Ms. Song turned to Brogan, her friendliness fading away as her tone became brusque. "You may collect your sample now, and then I need to conference with my clients, so you'll need to leave."

"You all suffer from a deplorable lack of manners." When no one replied to refute or own his words, he sniffed before reaching into a bag he set on the corner of Kade's desk, quickly removing a long swab and a vial in which to store it. "This is highly unusual."

"It's highly unusual for a CPS agent to be collecting a DNA sample in the field, too," said Ms. Song, her expression faintly suspicious.

"I already explained to the sheriff that it's a new policy we're instituting in San Francisco. It helps clear up identification issues much faster, so CPS agents in California are starting to carry DNA collection kits."

The attorney still looked skeptical. "It sounds like bad science to me to entrust it in the hands of people who have had very little training."

He glared at her as he opened the swab and approached Aislinn. "I'm certain I have far more scientific training than you do, Ms. Soong."

"Song," she corrected, looking unconcerned. "And do you really? Is science a big component of a social work degree?"

The CPS agent ignored her question as he focused on Aislinn. The baby tensed and squealed as he got nearer, and Shayla couldn't help wondering if the baby's bear instincts were kicking in to warn her that the man meant to do her harm, even benignly. Or perhaps she just didn't like strangers. She'd been so listless for so long that it was difficult to judge how she responded to people when she was feeling well. Now that she was feeling much better, and had made up for her growth deficiency plus some, perhaps she was just revealing more of her personality.

Either way, it was a struggle to get Aislinn to hold still long enough for Brogan to slip the cotton swab inside her mouth and take a sample from her cheek. As soon as he pulled away to cap the sample, she lifted Aislinn higher in her arms and jostled her gently, trying to avert a full-scale cry when the baby started whimpering. Fortunately, Aislinn seemed to be conducive to being soothed, and she was soon smiling again.

"You can leave us now," said Kade as soon as Brogan had the sample secured in his bag. "You know how to find the cabin I showed you."

"You mean the hovel," said Brogan with a snooty twist of his lips.

Kade shrugged. "You're lucky I'm not putting you out on the dock to wait for the next boat."

"I could still take control of the child."

"Actually, you can't," said Ms. Song in a pleasant tone. "The paperwork I've already given you includes the injunction against removing Aislinn before verifying her identity and state of health. As you well know."

Jeffrey Brogan sniffed at her as he gathered up his bag and marched from the office, not sparing another glance or word for any of them. His body language suggested petulance, and Shayla found it amusing that he was pouting over being thwarted. At least temporarily.

That thought brought a new rush of panic, and she turned to face the attorney. "Can you really protect Aislinn from him?"

She immediately nodded and firmly, looking completely confident. "I already have. We all know Aislinn is who we say she is, and the DNA will support that. Since she's back to good health, there is no reason for him to take custody of her. You're her guardian, and Kade will soon be listed on the birth certificate. I just need you to sign a couple of statements so I can file an amendment to the birth certificate." The attorney hesitated for a moment, trading an ambiguous glance with Kade.

"What?" Shayla's stomach clenched tightly.

"It's possible that your sister might face a little bit of legal trouble for lying on the birth certificate and the adoption paperwork. Kade has already offered to pay her legal fees if that happens, but it's only fair that you know the full consequences."

"Where do I sign?" Shayla felt bad about betraying Lila, but protecting Aislinn was far more important. The best way to do that was to ensure Kade could claim his daughter. She had to trust that Kade had meant what he said last night, and that he wasn't going to exclude her from Aislinn's life. Right now, she had to focus on protecting her niece from an overzealous CPS agent, and if that meant getting Lila in trouble, it would just have to be that way.

After reading through the documents, she signed them quickly while Kade held the baby, and then when he asked her to return to the cabin and stay there with Aislinn for the rest of the afternoon, she didn't hesitate. Perhaps she was being paranoid, but she thought it was safer to keep Aislinn out of view of the CPS man, and the cabin seemed like the safest place to do so.

9

Kade returned to the cabin that evening later than he had anticipated. It had taken a good part of the day to settle everything with Tru, including escorting her to the cabin Brogan had been assigned when they'd realized he hadn't left the DNA sample with her. Brogan hadn't been there, and it had taken a half-hour to track him down, finding him snooping through the town and interviewing people about their lifestyles. As Kade had gone behind him, he was surprised to learn the CPS agent had asked very few questions about Aislinn and far more about how they lived on the island.

At first, Brogan had been reluctant to hand over the DNA sample, insisting he wanted to send the test out to be performed by someone he trusted, but Kade and Tru had proven persuasive, if not more than a little threatening. Once she had the DNA sample in her bag, he had escorted her to the dock, where the boat she had arrived on had been moored, waiting for her. His friend Kingston had acted quickly, sending the best attorney his way and offering all the resources available to him for Kade's assistance. He had expressed his thanks via a message sent with Tru, and now he was finally returning to the cabin.

As he crossed the threshold, he paused at the sight before him. Shayla and Aislinn lay on the rug in front of the fireplace, both sleeping. The baby was wrapped in a towel, so she'd clearly had a bath. He was inferring Shayla had lain down with her in front of the fire to keep her warm, or perhaps simply to cuddle, and they had both fallen asleep. The firelight glowed on their faces, and in particular, it made Shayla's already-beautiful face breathtaking.

He was suddenly hard and aching for her, and he moved quietly as he lifted Aislinn from the floor, ensuring she didn't stir overly much as he carried her down the hall to his room, where he had fashioned a makeshift crib for her out of a dresser drawer. The bed in Shayla's room would have to do, because as much as he enjoyed the idea of making love to her in front of the fire, he didn't want his grandmother to walk in on them. He didn't think she would be overly upset, but it would be incredibly embarrassing for everyone.

With a strong amount of luck and a little finesse, he managed to put on a diaper and dress Aislinn in a sleeper without doing more than slightly rouse the baby. He rubbed her tummy, and she soon settled back to sleep. He hoped he'd have at least an hour or two before she woke ready to eat.

When he returned to the living room, he paused for just a moment again, standing over Shayla as he admired her sleep-softened face, and the soft waves flowing around her face. They'd probably be frizzy in no time, but he liked that. Hell, he liked everything about her, and he knew he'd been a fool by trying to deny the connection between them. She was meant to be his mate, and he should have surrendered to that the first time she walked into his office, rather than fighting it so hard.

Shayla was nothing like Lila, and their future would be completely different from the brief hell he'd endured with Lila, thanks to mistaking her for his mate. This time, he was certain there had been no mistake, and he strode forward to lift her from the floor much as he had done with Aislinn.

She stirred slightly but curled against him, her arms going around his neck seemingly in an automatic fashion. He snuggled closer to her, breathing in her sweet scent, and detected an underlying note of the honeysuckle soap his grandmother made. He had never smelled anything more exotic in all his life, and he could spend hours just breathing in her scent.

Or he could have if his jeans hadn't grown uncomfortably tight from her proximity and holding her curvy body in his arms.

He carried her back to her bedroom and laid her on the small bed, debating about whether he should do the gentlemanly thing and leave her to sleep, or if he should wake her up and ravish her. He was certain she'd be doing her own fair share of ravishing, too.

————

Shayla woke abruptly, opening her eyes and looking around with surprise to find herself in the guest room. The last thing she remembered was lying down by the fire with Aislinn, enjoying the warmth and a small cuddle. She must have been sleepier than she had realized, because she had dozed off.

Aislinn! What had happened to the baby?

Her gaze fell on Kade as she started to panic, and it

quickly abated. He must have taken care of her, but she still asked, "Where's the baby?"

"She's sleeping in my room."

She smiled at him, still feeling a little sleepy, but perfectly aware of what she was doing when she patted the small section of bed left beside her. "I guess that means you need somewhere else to sleep tonight?" They both knew that was silly, but it was the most blatant invitation she could manage as a small wave of shyness swept over her.

Kade didn't wait for a second invitation. She watched with amusement and appreciation for his fit form as he slipped off his clothes before sliding into bed with her. She wore only a plain nightgown she had slipped on after sharing a bath with Aislinn, and she was certain it would pose no barrier for Kade to extract her from it.

First, he cupped her face in his hands and brought his mouth to hers in a deep kiss. Their tongues dueled and mated, and the already-familiar taste of him washed over her, enhancing her arousal. She'd only kissed him one other time, but it felt like this was their millionth kiss, because it was so comfortable, but also completely unfamiliar. It was a strange juxtaposition, and it only heightened her desire for the man beside her.

The man and the bear. She reminded herself of the other side of him, though she really didn't need to. It lingered in the back of her mind that he was a bear-shifter, but she had decided to accept that, so she quickly banished all thought of it.

Kade kissed his way down from her mouth to her chin before moving lower to suck at the bend of her neck. She whimpered and stiffened against him, fingers tangling in his chest hair. She needed something to anchor herself as intense sensations swept through her body. Of course she'd had sex before, but this was different on every level. This meant something besides physical gratification, and though she had pictured or imagined herself in love before, she knew now it had been a pale imitation of the real thing.

She let out a small whimper as she realized she loved Kade. She wasn't certain how or when it had happened, but she was completely head-over-heels in love with him. It should have terrified her to feel so strongly for someone, especially so quickly, but instead, it felt right. It was as though she'd been waiting for Kade her entire life, and now that she'd found him, they clicked into place and fit together.

Was this the fate Tula had assured her she would believe in eventually?

Her fanciful thoughts faded as his touch grew bolder, and his mouth moved lower. He dealt with the buttons on her nightgown easily, leaving it open and her body available to him within seconds.

She buried her fingers in his hair and pulled his head more forcefully against her breast when he trailed the tip of his tongue over her taut nipple. She needed more than a teasing caress from him.

With a chuckle, which vibrated through her breast in a pleasing fashion, Kade complied with her request and began to suck more forcefully. It was almost too much pleasure, but she happily surrendered to it as he alternated his attention between that breast and the other, while his hands moved lower to explore all of her curves.

"Kade, I need you," she said in a broken voice when his fingers swept between her thighs, exploring the slickness of her slit and testing her readiness for him.

"You'll have me soon enough," he said as he lifted his head from her breast. His tongue trailed down her stomach as his body moved, and she marveled at how he contorted himself on the small bed. When he reached his destination a moment later, she couldn't think about anything except the pleasure he created with his tongue between her folds. She surrendered to the sensation, quickly overwhelmed by pleasure and the first of several orgasms as he expertly worked her with his tongue and mouth.

As he wrung yet another release from her, Shayla realized she was sobbing. It was mostly pleasure, but also a touch of exhaustion. "No more. Please, I can't do anymore."

He lifted his head, proof of her arousal on his face. "I'm sure you could, but I'll be merciful. For tonight." He winked at her as he moved up her body again.

Shayla wrapped her arms around him, just holding him close for a moment and savoring the feel of skin against skin. She could have fallen asleep like that, but the hard, insistent proof of his unsatisfied need reminded her he hadn't received the same pleasure. "Do you have any condoms? I didn't think to pack any."

Kade inhaled deeply. "You aren't ovulating."

She arched a brow. "That's a neat trick, but we should still use protection."

With a reluctant nod, he groaned softly before stirring. "It's in the other room. I'll be right back. Don't even think about moving." There was a gruff growl in his voice when he issued the warning.

She shifted slightly, feeling boneless. "I don't think I could if I wanted to—and I definitely don't want to."

He must have set a speed record, because he was back almost as soon as he had left, clutching a strip of condoms. She counted them quickly, eyes widening as she giggled. "You're optimistic."

He joined her on the bed again, ripping off one of the

condoms from the strip. "I'm not optimistic. I'm determined and driven. I waited too long for you to be satisfied with just once tonight."

As he sheathed himself in latex, she shifted on the bed to make the position easier and her body more welcoming to him. "It does seem like I've been waiting for this forever, and I didn't even know I was looking for it."

Kade settled between her thighs, guiding his shaft to her opening, before gently sliding inside. He went slowly, because he was large, and she was unaccustomed to a lover of his size.

Once he was fully inside her, Kade remained buried there for a few moments, neither rocking their hips as their gazes locked while their bodies fused. It was an intimate moment, and about far more than sex. They were connecting on a level she hadn't even known existed, and she clung to him as he began to slowly thrust in and out of her. It was uncomfortable for a moment or two, but she soon adjusted and welcomed each surge of his cock inside her.

Shayla dug her fingers into his buttocks, wanting every bit of him, and they strained together, thrusts growing rapidly erratic. She had been convinced she couldn't orgasm again that night, so it was with some surprise she felt herself falling over the edge a few minutes later, preceding Kade's release by milliseconds. She convulsed around him as his shaft twitched inside her, and they clung to each other fiercely as pleasure ravaged them while binding them even tighter together.

10

S hayla made no effort to hide her grimace of dismay when Tula led Jeffrey Brogan into the small cabin two days later after answering a knock at the door.

She knew from Kade that the man had spent the last two days snooping around the island and interrogating people who crossed his path, asking questions about their life and their family history, which was pretty odd considering he was supposed to be there because of Aislinn. She was unsurprised that he had finally made his way back to them, and she braced herself for another round of questions.

She quickly realized she wasn't the only one on-edge. Brogan appeared twitchy, looking over his shoulder frequently and jumping at the smallest sound. It was strange behavior, and her frown deepened.

"May I have some coffee?" he asked Tula.

Tula looked put out by the idea, but she gave him a grudging nod as she got to her feet again from her chair and headed to the kitchen to make him a cup of coffee. "I hope you like instant," she called over her shoulder. "I don't have anything fancy here."

Shayla barely stifled a grin, knowing the older woman was fibbing. There was a nice Keurig machine in the kitchen, along with a selection of gourmet coffees. Clearly, Tula had deemed him unworthy of her collection of assorted brews, and Shayla concurred.

As Tula bustled into the kitchen, Brogan's gaze moved to Aislinn. "It really is her, isn't it?"

Instinctively, she tightened her arms around the baby. "Of course it's Aislinn."

"I don't need DNA to tell me that, not after what I've observed the last couple of days. These people are remarkable, and I shouldn't be surprised at how quickly their offspring grows."

Shayla frowned at the words, alarmed by how clinical they sounded, and also suggesting he knew more about the people on the island than he was supposed to. Had he somehow learned they were bear-shifters? It seemed like a preposterous idea, but she couldn't rule it out with his strange behavior. She chose not to reply.

"This is such an amazing opportunity. I arrived at the island expecting to find the child on the verge of death. I'd hoped I would arrive in time to perform an autopsy and collect samples, so it was a wondrous surprise to discover she's alive and thriving. Just think what we can learn from her."

Shayla frowned at him. "What are you talking about? Why would the CPS want to do an autopsy on my baby, even if she had been on the verge of death?"

He gave her a censorious look. "I'm sure you've figured out by now that I'm not with CPS, Ms. Dalton. I'm actually the scientist who ran the DNA tests that your doctor submitted to the state lab. I knew right away there was something different and unusual about the child, and I wanted to know more. To protect the scientific find, I sent back falsified results that reveal nothing officially about her strange genetics. I really need to study her before I can take this finding public."

Shayla stiffened her spine and pointed to the door. "Get out. You have no business here and no authority, so leave us alone."

Brogan, if that was his real name, clicked his tongue at her. "Don't be so shortsighted. Think of others, and what we can glean from the shifters' DNA. They rapidly heal, they seem to live long and healthy lives, and they're impervious to most diseases. You could help me find the potential in their DNA to share with humans, too. Just give me the child, and I assure you she'll be used only for the highest scientific principles."

Her mouth dropped open, and she stared at him in shocked disbelief. "Do you really think I'm going to just hand over my daughter because of the nonsense you're spouting? I already told you to leave. Get out now."

His pleasant smile faded, and his tone was chiding when he spoke again. "I'm disappointed in your inability to see the potential in this matter. No matter though. I expected such a reaction. Give me the child, and I won't hurt you."

Tula returned with his cup of coffee, just in time to hear the last words he spoke. "Have you managed to lift the injunction the attorney placed against you?"

"No, he hasn't, Tula." She rubbed Aislinn's back as the baby began to fuss. "He's not really with the CPS. He's a scientist who wants to study Aislinn's unique DNA."

A growl emanated from Tula, and the cup she'd been holding hit the floor as her body started to enlarge. "Get out."

"That's what I said," said Shayla. "He seems hard-of-hearing though, because he's still here."

Tula paused in mid-shift as Brogan removed a gun from his suit jacket's pocket, holding it focused squarely on Aislinn. "Let's not be hasty. Obviously, I prefer the child alive for long-term study, but even tissue samples will aid me in unraveling the DNA. You can hand her over and be assured I'll look after her, or you can all die here. Be sensible."

Tula completed her transformation as he finished speaking, rising on her back paws to tower over him.

Considering how twitchy he had been previously, he seemed remarkably unaffected by the sight of the human/bear-shifter looming over him. He switched his target from Aislinn to Tula, firing without hesitation. Tula grunted at the impact of the bullet, but she lumbered on toward him. He fired three more times before the old woman stopped, dropping first to all fours and then to the floor with a small whine of pain.

Shayla wanted to rush to her to check on Tula, but she couldn't make herself move as the gun returned to her and Aislinn, this time focusing squarely on her. She wanted to call his bluff, but it seemed pretty obvious he wasn't bluffing. She had no idea how many bullets remained in his gun, but he must have a fairly sizable caliber if four shots had been enough to incapacitate Tula. She glanced away briefly from Brogan and the gun to look at Tula, reassured when she saw her sides heaving, though the strange breathing was a concern.

"Don't worry. I'm sure she'll survive. She's just down for a bit. I need the child now so I have time to get away before she's up and around, or that Kade fellow can return and stop me. Hand her over."

She glared at the scientist, shaking her head. "You're not getting my baby."

He let out a sharp sigh. "Don't you understand that you won't recover the same way these people do will if I shoot you? You'll be dead. Be sensible and hand over the child."

"Over my dead body."

He seemed to lose the last shred of patience as he strode forward, pressing the gun against her forehead even though she tried to rear back. She was pinned against the wall, and there was nowhere to go. Shayla clung to Aislinn anyway. "You can't have her."

He let out a sound of frustration before swinging his arm back. At first, she thought he was adjusting the aim of his bullet, but she realized he was choosing a different route as the gun approached her temple at a rapid pace.

She tried to flinch away, but there really was nowhere to go. The hard, cold metal connected with her head, and she could feel consciousness slipping away in a matter of seconds. Her arms loosened their hold on Aislinn, and she felt Brogan pulling the baby from her. Shayla summoned the last of her strength and tried to hold on, but when he hit her again with the gun, she was completely out that time.

***

K ade let out a roar, barely holding back the urge to shift to his bear form when he entered the cabin and found his grandmother injured and Shayla unconscious. Aislinn was nowhere in sight. He wasn't alone, so he sent Jamie Scarborough to check on his grandmother as he rushed across the room to Shayla.

His hands shook as he searched for a pulse, convinced he might not find one from all the blood pouring down the side of her head. Relief swept through him when he found a strong pulse seconds later. It seemed to indicate she would make a full recovery, but he was no doctor. He stroked her face, hoping she would waken soon, as he looked over at Jamie and his grandmother.

Tula had shifted back to her human form, and in doing so, bullets had popped out of her body. They lay scattered on the rag rug, and the holes in her body were rapidly healing. She looked gaunt and gray, and he knew she needed protein quickly. He didn't have to tell Jamie that, because the younger man was already rushing to the refrigerator in search of something that would aid Tula's healing.

"It was that CPS agent," rasped Tula as Jamie returned to her with a slab of raw salmon.

Kade grimaced. "He's no CPS agent. I don't know what he is, but he's not with Child Protective Services. Tru initiated the DNA test, and she also started digging into the investigation, only to discover there isn't one, and there is no Jeffrey Brogan working for CPS."

"He's a scientist," said a reed-thin voice.

Another surge of relief swept through Kade as she spoke. He turned to look at Shayla again, a ragged exhale escaping him when he saw the alertness in her eyes. "What kind of scientist?" His mouth seemed to form the question independently of his brain, because his thoughts were consumed with finding Aislinn and breaking Brogan in half for what he'd done to his family.

"I don't know if he's a lab technician or a geneticist, but he ran the DNA tests on Aislinn and realized she was special. He buried the information so he could take advantage of it himself, ostensibly for noble scientific purposes, but probably because he sees dollar signs when he looks at our baby."

The few sentences seemed to have exhausted Shayla, and she slumped against the wall more than she had even a few seconds ago. Kade leaned forward and picked her up carefully, moving her from the floor to the couch as he accepted a handful of paper towels Jamie had brought him without him needing to ask.

He pressed them carefully against the side of her head, where two deep gashes continued to release a steady flow of blood. "I'm going to send the doctor to look at you, and then I want you to stay in the cabin. I'm going to find our daughter. I promise you that."

"No, I want to come with you. I can hold her when you find her."

He let out a small sigh. "I understand you want to be there for her, but I don't think you can even stand up right now. You'll just slow us down. I don't mean to be brutal, but we need to move quickly and find him before he gets off the island."

She seemed reluctant, but she stopped arguing. "I guess you're right."

He winked at her. "I'm always right. It's good that you're realizing that now."

"If my head wasn't pounding, I'd roll my eyes. Go find our daughter."

"I should wait with you until the doctor arrives."

It seemed to take a large measure of strength for her to lift a hand and waive it vaguely in the air. "I don't think you have to worry about us. We're not his target. I'm particularly not his target, because I'm just human. He's not interested in me, and Tula is still recovering, so she's no threat to him. He won't be back here. I think it's obvious he has some escape plan in mind, so you need to get her before he gets away from Bear Island."

Kade accepted the wisdom of her words with a brief nod, though it went against his instincts to leave his injured mate behind. He turned to Jamie. "Get Doc Buroh here right away, and don't leave them after you've fetched her. Your job is to protect my mate and my grandmother."

The younger man nodded, looking slightly nervous at the prospect, though his chest puffed out with pride at being selected for such an important task. Kade didn't have it in him to remind the kid that he was the only one available at the moment.

He pressed a tender kiss to the side of Shayla's head that wasn't bleeding before standing fully erect. "I'll be back soon with Aislinn."

He didn't wait for a response as he rushed from the cabin, shedding his clothes as he did so. As soon as he cleared the steps, he shifted to his bear form, his senses instantly heightened. He could smell everything a thousand times better now, and he had little trouble picking up Brogan's scent and following his trail. He also picked up other members of the clan, as they shifted and joined behind him. They might not know exactly what was going on, but they sensed danger and were responding by providing him support and backup.

He quickly realized during Brogan's snooping, the man must have discovered the small cove at the edge of the island where they kept a few boats in case of an emergency. It was separate from their main marina, where they had three larger boats that could accommodate everyone on the island in the need of evacuation. These were used for shorter trips or smaller groups of people. They were decked out as fishing boats, though none of his people needed to use a boat to fish. It was far more efficient to go swimming in the ocean and catch a fish in bear-form.

Realizing his destination, Kade increased his already-brutal pace until he could feel his muscles burning. He wasn't concerned about Brogan being able to escape, because any of them could probably swim long enough to catch up with the motors on the boats.

What worried him was the idea of Brogan taking an infant out on the open sea in one of the small fishing boats. It was a glorified motorboat, and it certainly wasn't up for a long trip, like the distance to Seattle. He also didn't know Brogan's level of boating experience, but assumed it couldn't be much if the man thought it was safe to take a motorboat across the Strait to get back to Seattle. He'd run out of gas halfway there, and unless he took oars, he'd be stranded there.

For his part, Kade didn't care if the man was stuck in the middle of the ocean until he starved to death, but he wasn't going to let his daughter be a casualty.

He caught up with Brogan near the top of the bluff. Brogan hadn't begun the descent down the side that would take him to the small cove, so Kade shifted into his human form in order to speak. "Stop now, and give me back my daughter. It's over, Brogan. You can still walk away, but you can't take Aislinn."

The man teetered at the edge of the cliff for a moment, clearly startled by Kade's words and presence. He glanced behind him, meeting Kade's gaze. "I have everything riding on this. Prestige, scientific inquiry, and possibly even a Nobel prize. I'm afraid I need the child. You can always have another."

A chorus of growls accompanied his insensitive words,

but Kade's was still issued in his human voice. The others were definitely from bears.

Brogan seemed to realize at that moment that it wasn't just Kade he was facing. His eyes widened in the rapidly approaching twilight as he took in the sight of multiple bears standing behind Kade. Kade had no idea how many of his people had joined him, but he knew it must be an impressive or terrifying sight, depending on one's perspective. "Give me the baby."

Kade sensed Brogan's hesitation and uncertainty, and he also realized from the other man's body language and the scent of fear rolling off him that he was panicking. That close to the edge of the cliff, it was a recipe for disaster, and Kade gave up on the idea of a cautious approach. He shifted back as he began to run, certain Brogan would be going over the cliff any moment, either from panic or from Kade's assistance. First, he had to get to Aislinn.

Jeffrey started to topple backward just as Kade reached him. He used a paw to hook on to Brogan's shoulder, his claws keeping the other man from falling, though the scientist screamed from the pain.

Kade ignored his cries as he used his other paw to gently extract Aislinn from Brogan's tight hold. When she was freed, he set her carefully down on the ground as far away as he could reach, aware of someone from his clan moving behind him in human form to whisk the baby to safety.

Jeffrey was windmilling his arms, and his body wasn't at all secure. He continued to slide backward, and only Kade's claws kept him from falling. "Let me go. Let me go," he shouted again. "Don't hurt me."

Kade supposed his conscience should twinge, but he didn't experience even a small dart of guilt as he retracted his claws and complied with Brogan's demand that he let him go.

Brogan screamed as he started to fall, but his cries didn't last long. He collided with the rocky outcropping below, less than ten feet from one of the fishing boats that would have secured his escape, or at least allowed him to get partway to Seattle and off Bear Island.

Kade turned away from the gruesome sight of his broken body, certain the other man couldn't have survived that. He'd have to deal with it soon enough, but first, he needed to get Aislinn back to her mother and assure himself they were both fine. He was certain his grandmother had healed by now, but he wanted to check on her too.

At that moment, his family took precedence over the body of the man who had tried to tear it apart.

11

Three days later, Kade decided, mostly due to her own insistence, that Shayla had healed enough to accept his mating bite. It was just the two of them in his bedroom, since Tula had volunteered to take the baby for the night. She'd had a gleam in her eye that revealed she knew exactly what was so special about tonight, and she clearly approved.

Kade kissed Shayla again, his hands roaming over her soft curves before delving between her thighs. She was slick with need, but he held himself back another moment, wanting to be sure she knew what was coming. "And you understand why I'm going to bite you?"

She nodded, looking unconcerned. "It's so your scent will be on me, and others will know we're mated." Shayla quirked a brow. "I think it's unnecessary though. I can't imagine any of your clan trying to claim me. They all hate me."

He growled. "They don't. They're wary of outsiders, but they've already accepted you."

She nodded, seeming to remember the outpouring from

the community in the past few days, with numerous offerings of food, companionship, and childcare forthcoming from the people who had been like ghosts around her until that point. "I hope you're right. I know you are," she said more firmly. "Either way, I'm okay with you marking me as yours to ward off the other horny bear-shifters."

"That's the practical side of it, but it's also pleasurable for both of us." He could see her skepticism, and he couldn't blame her. The idea of being bitten probably sounded frightening, but he had already explained the procedure to her, and she seemed excited, if a little frightened.

He couldn't resist any longer, so he moved between her thighs and slid his cock inside her, making them both cry out with satisfaction at being joined together. After establishing a rhythm that pleased both of them, Kade gathered her close to him and buried his face against the bend of her neck. As she started to tighten around him a few minutes later, heralding the approach of her release, he barely held his own in check, wanting to be sure she received her pleasure first.

When her convulsions increased around him, and he was certain she was coming, he surrendered to his own orgasm with a hoarse shout and allowed his teeth to elongate slightly as he did so. He bit her shoulder, not hard enough to draw blood, but deep enough to mark her with his scent. As he'd expected, rather than detracting from her pleasure, it seemed to increase the intensity of her orgasm, and she almost screamed his name as she tightened around him, fingers clawing against his buttocks to pull him deeper inside her.

He was already as far as he could go, and he clung to her as the last pulses of his seed left him. He knew she wasn't ovulating, but the idea of her carrying his baby filled his chest with warmth. Due to quicker pregnancies among his kind, they could give Aislinn a sibling seven months after Shayla began ovulating.

Afterward, they collapsed together in a sweating heap, properly mated for the first time. A wave of satisfaction swept through him, and this one was deeper than sexual release. He was satisfied to his soul and content in a way he'd never been before. "I love you, Shayla."

She was panting slightly, still recovering from the intense bout of lovemaking, so he was unsurprised when it took her a moment to reply. "Love you, too," she said in a slightly broken voice.

He liked the idea of breaking her with passion and putting her back together with love. She could do the same to him anytime. He curled up against her, and with his mate in his arms, Kade slept deeper than he had in years.

BONUS EXCERPT: ONE NIGHT WITH A BEAR

Jade braced herself as the gawky young man who'd been eyeing her for the last twenty minutes seemed to work up the nerve to approach. She had come to the bar hoping for some companionship, but this guy had to be at least ten years her junior, and he reminded her of the kids she taught at the university every day. There was no way it was going to happen, and she'd hope that by ignoring him, it would take care of itself. No such luck.

He sat down at the bar beside her, all fake confidence and swagger, slamming his empty glass onto the bar. That earned him an annoyed look from the bartender, and she barely bit back a giggle when the kid flinched. He wasn't quite the stud he pretended to be. It softened her slightly toward him. Not enough to actually accept any of his overtures, but she'd try to be gentle with her letdown.

"Hey, how you doing?"

She managed a neutral nod, thinking he sounded so much like that old character on "Friends." What was his name? Joey, that was the one. It had been years since she'd seen that show, and she had a feeling this kid had never seen it unless he'd watched it on Netflix. "I'm fine." She didn't inquire about him, hoping to cut short the conversation.

Apparently, the kid just didn't get subtlety. "May I buy you a drink?"

She looked down at her mostly full Bloody Mary. "I'm good."

He was starting to look shaky, and she was amused when he shot a glance over his shoulder. She could well imagine his friends at the table were giving him a thumbs-up or other signs of encouragement, delusional young men that they were.

"Do you come here often?"

Jade shrugged. "Upon occasion. It's close to work." Which also meant it was close to the university, which was a downside. She really had picked the wrong bar this evening if she'd hoped to meet someone to take home.

"Where do you work?" His eyes gleamed with excitement suddenly. "Do you work at that strip club across the street?"

She let out a genuine laugh as she gave her curvy body a rueful glance. She imagined there would certainly be a market for curvy strippers, but that was outside her field of expertise. "No, not at all. I work at the university."

The bartender had brought him a fresh glass, but he showed no sign of taking his beer back to his table. "What do you do there?"

"I'm a professor of archaeology."

He suddenly looked slightly ashen. "A professor?"

She gave him a smile, though it didn't reach her eyes. "Yes. Didn't I have you last semester?" She was certain she hadn't, but she was hoping to emphasize the age difference to the young man without having to brutally shoot him down.

He gulped his beer, looking like he might choke on it for a moment. "No, I don't think so. I haven't taken an archaeology class yet."

"You go to the university then?"

He nodded again. "Yeah. First year," he mumbled, as though embarrassed by the revelation.

She winced slightly, having pegged him at least a few years older than that. It was a good thing she wasn't a cougar. She couldn't help frowning at the glass of beer in his hand. "Aren't you a bit young for that then?" She asked the question quietly, so as not to rouse the bartender's interest. He was busy with the group that had recently entered anyway, and they looked as out-of-place as she felt tonight. In their leather and denim, they seemed to scream biker gang, and she wondered how they'd ended up at this bar.

He shrugged, looking defensive. "I'm twenty-one."

"Of course you are," she said dryly.

The kid stopped making any further attempts to pick her up after that. He took his drink and slunk back to his table, where she was certain his friends commiserated with him, and perhaps pointed out he'd had a lucky break by avoiding the old broad. No, those kids probably didn't use the word broad at all. She didn't know exactly what they would call her, and she was fine with that. She didn't aspire to be the cool professor, and she didn't much care about what was hip or popular among the younger kids.

Wow, she was starting to sound like an old curmudgeon. Here she was, only thirty-two, and already set in her ways. She might as well embrace spinsterhood and buy at least ten cats if she kept on this path.

The idea of packing up ten cats to take with her to her next dig site was a ludicrous idea, and she almost giggled aloud. She would have if she hadn't looked up at just the right moment to see a new person entering the bar. She could tell right away he was part of the biker group, or at least meeting them, since he wore sinfully tight jeans, a crisp white t-shirt, and a leather vest. It wasn't his outfit that garnered her attention though.

It was, bluntly, his smoking hot body to start with. He had muscular thighs, and she was certain his stomach would be flat as a washboard with a well-defined six-pack. She found herself idly wondering if he would have a lot of chest hair or just a little bit. She decided he'd be on the slightly hairy side, but she didn't know why she thought that.

Her gaze swept higher, and her eyes locked with his. His eyes were the shade of the ocean at midday and fringed by thick blond lashes. He had scruff on his cheeks, and his hair was slightly overgrown. He had the careless renegade look down perfectly, but she was convinced it wasn't an affectation. She doubted he had spent hours going for the look. Rather, it had just occurred naturally for him.

She was embarrassed when her nipples hardened against the lace of her bra, and she had to resist the self-conscious urge to cross her arms over her chest to hide proof of her sudden arousal.

She held her breath as she waited to see if he would approach her, and she refused to acknowledge the wave of disappointment that swept through her when he turned away from her to meet his friends instead. Clearly, the interest had been one-sided. Feeling glum, she finished the rest of her drink and dropped a few bills on the bar. This was turning out to be a disaster of a night, and she really should head home to get some sleep since her flight left early the next morning.

She was just about to climb off the stool when she realized he was standing behind her. She turned slowly, looking over her shoulder and up at him. Way up. He was a big, solid man, and though she was curvy, she had a feeling he could pick her up easily. The thought might have alarmed her from anyone else, but the idea of him doing it only excited her.

"Leaving already?" It was a rough growl more than syllables.

She shrugged a shoulder. "I have an early flight."

"Join me for a drink first." It wasn't exactly an invitation. It was more like a demand coated in velvet, but his body language made it clear he wasn't letting her go just yet.

If she hadn't been so attracted to him, she would have found his attitude insufferable. She normally would anyway, but there was just something about him that made her want to comply. He didn't need to know that though. "You're awfully bossy."

His chiseled lips twitched, and he inclined his head. "Guilty as charged."

She didn't resist when he took her hand and led her to a table in the corner, one that would give them some privacy. Her heart raced at the touch of his hand, and she found it difficult to draw in a deep breath. She was either really attracted to him, or she was about to have a pulmonary embolism.

They sat together, and she realized neither one of them had ordered drinks. Apparently, that didn't matter, because the bartender quickly arrived with drinks for both of them. It was the first time she'd seen him leave the bar all night.

He usually made the patrons come to him. Was he responding to the stranger's commanding presence too?

"Another Bloody Mary for the lady, and your usual, Cody."

As the bartender stepped away, her eyes widened with surprise. "You're a regular here?"

He took a sip of his beer before responding. "Would that surprise you?"

She shrugged. "It's more of a college hangout than a biker bar."

He grinned. "Yes, it is. The bartender's my nephew though."

She looked back at the young man behind the bar before glancing at him again. "He can't be much younger than you are."

He shook his head. Cody was what the bartender called him. Cody shook his head. He looked like a Cody.

She was mentally rambling like a moron.

"I'm about ten years older than he is. I was a late baby and a big surprise for my mom and dad, and all my brothers are older than me. After six boys already, they thought they were done, but along came me. Then my oldest brother had my nephew a few years after I was born."

She took a sip of the Bloody Mary, finding it just as perfect as the last one. "So your mom had seven boys? How many girls?"

"None. Girls aren't born in our family very often, for some reason." He shrugged. "My nephew Kade and his mate...wife bucked that trend though. They have a little girl and another one on the way."

She found the idea of such a large family fascinating, but that was probably because she'd grown up as an only child. Like Cody, she'd been a surprise late baby for her parents, though neither one of them had really ever wanted to have children. Her mother had been forty-seven when she was born, and far too old and set in her ways to understand or indulge a young child.

Madeline Barnes had happily entrusted her care to the nanny and gone about her life as usual. Frank Barnes had been just as absorbed in his own academic career, and she hadn't seen much of her parents at all until she was older, had learned her manners, and knew to always be quiet and polite around them, and never behave like a child. It must have been amazing to grow up with so many siblings, even if they were older than Cody.

She was envious for a moment, and she nearly confessed her own wish to have a large family—a desire that seemed less likely as the years passed. While she could conceivably have children for at least ten more years, she wasn't certain she wanted to have them that close together. And discussing the family she wanted with a potential one-night stand seemed like the best way to send him running, which she didn't want.

For that matter, the prospect of having any children was pretty dim at the moment. She couldn't seem to find a man who interested her or could put up with her own eccentricities for longer than a few weeks. She'd been in such a long dry spell that it was practically a drought, and that was unlikely to change in the next four months when she was at the dig site. She'd be surrounded by eager young students, and perhaps a colleague or two, but no one who made her heart race the way this man did. "What was it like growing up with all those brothers?"

Cody shrugged. "They were a lot older than me, like I said, so I think I annoyed the hell out of them as I tagged along. They were good about watching out for me though, and we're still close. We're closer now that I'm an adult and no longer that annoying little brother."

"What were you like as a kid?"

"Always in trouble." He made the admission with a charming grin.

It provoked a smile of her own in response. "Oddly enough, I imagine you're telling me the truth."

He gave her a cocky grin. "I don't lie."

"Ever?"

He shrugged. "I try not to."

She snorted. "Everybody tells lies. Just the little ones maybe, like if I asked you do these pants make my butt look fat, you're going to say no, of course not. We both know they do, but I don't care because they're comfortable." Skinny jeans weren't necessarily an invention intended for women of her size, but she didn't care. She liked them, so she wore them.

There was a new level of heat in his eyes when he raked his gaze over her again. "Honestly, I can't see your butt from here, but from what I remember as you got off the barstool, it was a luscious ass, and those jeans are perfect for it."

She almost choked on the drink in her mouth, not having expected that. "You're a smooth one."

"I'm just being honest. You asked me what I thought of your ass, and I'm telling you it's about the best one I've ever seen."

She blushed like a schoolgirl, which was embarrassing in itself. "Actually, I mentioned my jeans, and not my ass. I mean I wasn't asking for your opinion of my ass."

Cody sipped his beer before responding. "I guess you can have my opinion for free then. The ass is spectacular, as is the rest of the package. You're a beautiful woman, and I don't even know your name."

She giggled before abruptly cutting off the juvenile sound. "I'm sorry. We haven't been formally introduced. I heard the bartender call you Cody, but I forgot to give you my name." She held out her hand, unsurprised when she found his fingers and palm rough from hard work. It was a pleasant feel and a nice contrast to the usual hands she shook in her daily academic life. "I'm Dr. Jade Barnes."

He looked impressed. "You're a doctor, huh? I've got this spot I'd like you to look at." His eyes twinkled as they darted down to his lap before looking up at her again.

She shook her head. "Sorry, but that's the wrong kind of doctor. I have a PhD in archaeology, and I'm a professor at the university."

"I still have a spot I'd like you to look at."

She couldn't hold in a laugh. "I still say you're a smooth talker, whether or not you're being honest."

"I assure you I'm being completely honest about the spot I'd like you to see. You have some spots I'd like to see too. See, touch, and taste." This time, there was no teasing his expression. "Do you want to get out of here?"

Did she? There was hardly a space between him asking and her answering. "Yes, very much." She had come to the bar this evening with the half-formed idea of picking up someone if the opportunity arose, since she was sure to be out of social contact for the next few months, starting tomorrow.

It had been more than a year since the last time she'd been with a man, and that had been a brief, disastrous relationship. She wasn't after a relationship. This was just sex, and though she wasn't accustomed to one-night stands, not having one since college, she decided to go for it tonight. What was the worst that could happen?

Immediately, she realized he could be a serial killer, but

she quickly discarded that notion. She couldn't explain it, but she trusted Cody. Perhaps it was because she believed he really was an honest man, or perhaps it was because she wanted him so badly that she was fooling herself. Whatever it was, she barely had any second thoughts as she followed him out of the bar and across the road to a hotel bearing the logo of a national chain.

She rented the room, uncertain of his financial status. That didn't matter to her anyway, especially for just one night, but she wasn't positive he could afford it. She supposed that was a snobbish assumption, and the kind of judgment her parents would make, but she shrugged it off. She had good intentions, and even if she found out he had filed bankruptcy ten times in a row, it didn't matter for what she wanted from him. Just sex, she reminded herself as she took the key card, and they walked together to the elevator.

As soon as they stepped inside, she realized the compartment felt smaller than usual. Cody had a way of dominating the space and seeming to suck up all the oxygen. That was the only explanation for her sudden breathlessness. Either that, or his proximity. Either way, it was his fault.

She half-expected him to touch her in the elevator, even in just a casual way, but he kept his hands to himself and stayed on his side of the elevator, much to her disappointment. She was too old for a grope session in the elevator, but it suddenly seemed like a fun idea with this man.

Fortunately, they were on the third floor, so the ride took only a few seconds. The desk clerk had given them a room near the elevator, and she reminded herself to give him a large tip if she saw him again. Perhaps he recognized two horny people in desperate need of each other and had done his best to make it easy on them.

More likely, it had simply been the next available room, but she rather liked the idea of thinking there were outside forces at work that had arranged this night for them. It was a fanciful thought for a professor who didn't believe in anything she couldn't see, touch, taste, or hear. She didn't believe in fate, but a man like Cody made her want to.

The room was nicely furnished, if average and nondescript. It had everything they needed, which was basically the bed.

As soon as the door closed behind them, Cody reached for her. All the anticipation of the evening rushed through her, leaving her head spinning as he put his arms around her. He was even more solid than she had guessed, and it was like embracing a stone pillar as he held her against him. He smelled like pine and something uniquely male, and his lips were softer than she had guessed when they molded to hers. His stubble was scratchy, but in a pleasant way, and she opened her mouth to yield to his questing tongue.

He kissed like he did everything else, in a forceful and commanding way. He demanded her submission, and she had no trouble granting it. It was completely unlike her, but she surrendered to the impulse, allowing Cody to take the lead.

They continued kissing as he moved her inexorably backward toward the bed, and she didn't even realize he was maneuvering her that way until her knees hit the mattress, causing her to fall onto her bum on the soft mattress. She let out a small squeal of surprise, but he quickly swallowed the sound as he deepened the kiss. He twined his hands in her blonde hair, holding her tightly against him as though afraid she would slip away if given the chance. She had no intention of going anywhere, and to prove it, she clung to his shoulders, urging him closer.

He seemed to have magic fingers and had soon unbuttoned her top and pushed it off her shoulders. In contrast, hers were fumbling with the zipper on his vest. It should have been an easy task, yet she couldn't seem to manage it.

"Leave it," he growled, taking her hand away. It was an inpatient gesture, but she intuited it came from his desperate need for her, rather than him being annoyed at her difficulty with removing his garment.

Cody stood up for a moment, seeming to be reluctant to part from her. She felt the same way, and she took advantage of him stripping off his clothes to do the same with her own. It was a bit unnerving to get naked with a stranger, but as Cody returned to her, gathering her into his arms again, she realized he didn't feel like a stranger. It was different to have such an instant connection with someone, and she tried to shrug it off, assuring herself it was just sex. That's all she wanted or needed from him.

Cody pushed her back onto the bed, his mouth finally wandering from hers to move down her body. He took one firm nipple into his mouth, sucking gently while his hand cupped her other breast. His fingers glided around her nipple, tugging intermittently, and she moaned at the sensation. She was already more excited than she'd ever been with another man, and she could only imagine how it would be when they actually had sex. She couldn't wait to feel him inside her—on the other hand, she was in no hurry to speed up the foreplay either. Especially since his mouth was so good at what it was doing.

That mouth decided to travel farther down, and her stomach fluttered with excitement as his tongue trailed over her abdomen before moving lower, and he paused at the apex of her thighs. She shivered when he buried his face against her, breathing in her scent. She was convinced that's what he was doing, and it seemed strange, but also sexy as hell.

"Mine," he said in a gruff voice before his mouth covered her. His tongue slid between her folds, and he immediately sought out her neglected clit. Jade grasped handfuls of his overly long hair, pinning him closer to her body. He chuckled against her core, making her lower half twitch, and she arched against him in a demanding fashion.

Cody didn't seem to mind complying with her request, and he began to lick faster. His tongue probed all of her parts, learning everything about her sheath and soon bringing her to the edge of orgasm. He held her there for a moment, not allowing her to slip over. He stopped moving his tongue and stopped sucking.

"Please," she whimpered. With a small laugh, he darted out his tongue and flicked it under the hood of her clit, which sent her flying completely over the edge.

As she was coming down from her orgasm, she was vaguely aware of him moving off the bed again to retrieve something from his pants. As she heard the foil packet tear, she realized he had gone for a condom. Thankfully he had the foresight to use one, because she was so caught up in the bliss of the moment that she would have happily taken him inside her and not even thought about the consequences until much later.

It should have been a wake-up call, but she was too far immersed in how she was feeling and how much she wanted Cody to worry about how deeply in she was already. Instead, she held out her arms and welcomed him back to her, taking the condom from him and sliding it on his shaft herself. Her eyes widened slightly as she realized just how large he was, and she gulped quietly. It was a good thing she wasn't a virgin, or this never would have worked.

"Are you ready for me, baby?" He seemed to ask the question through gritted teeth, as though he were in pain. Perhaps he was, finding it as difficult to hold back as she was.

She nodded. "More than ready. Are you?"

He looked to be in pain, as though her question had caused him physical suffering. "I was ready from the moment I smelled you across the bar."

She frowned at that. "Do I stink?"

He chuckled. "No, not at all. You smell amazing."

It was a strange compliment, but she was more than happy to take it, just like his cock. Still holding it in her hands, she guided him to her opening before letting go. She moved her hands to his back and wrapped her thighs around his waist as he sank into her. They began to thrust against each other, slowly at first, but soon caught up in the passion of the moment.

The pace of his thrusts increased, and she moved her hands to his buttocks, digging in her nails lightly to encourage him to take all of her. She had been concerned about his size, but once he was inside her, it was as though they were made to fit each other. She wanted more of him, so she increased the pace of her hips, and he responded. Soon, they were clinging to each other as they orgasmed simultaneously. She'd never done that with a lover before, and to achieve it with what was essentially a one-night stand with someone she barely knew was a strange turn of events.

Somehow, she was unsurprised though. It just felt right with Cody. Everything felt right with him, which was slightly alarming, since this was only one night. Just sex, she reminded herself as they indulged in more. It was a long night, and she was going to be exhausted on her plane ride tomorrow, but she couldn't find it in herself to care or worry about the practicalities at the moment. She was too absorbed in Cody.

***

Sometime near dawn, they fell asleep, and he was still inside her. That felt right too, but it proved awkward when she woke an hour later, the alarm on her watch alerting her that it was time to get up and get ready for her flight. She still had to go home and grab her bag, and she didn't have time to shower or to have a long, drawn-out goodbye with her one-night stand. She couldn't imagine it was Cody's style anyway, and he would probably appreciate her slipping quietly away into the night without the fuss of a morning-after postmortem of the night before.

Gingerly, she pulled away from him, squirming across the bed until she could swing free and get up. She waited to see if he had awakened, but he was snoring softly. She had worn him out, but as a wave of exhaustion swept over her, she knew it was a mutual effect they'd had on each other. She was definitely going to sleep most of the day on the plane.

She dressed quickly, finding as many of her clothes as possible. The location of her bra was a mystery, so she left it behind. She felt like she was sneaking out, and she supposed she was, but she was saving them both any awkwardness. That was how these things worked, right? She hadn't had a one-night stand since college, but she remembered the awkwardness of the morning after, when the guy had offered her breakfast he clearly didn't want to fix, and she hadn't been able to get dressed fast enough.

She'd regretted that night, but she was certain she wouldn't regret anything about the one she'd spent with Cody, except perhaps the duration. One night didn't seem like nearly enough, but there were no other alternatives. She still didn't know his last name, and she was going to be out of town for four months. By the time she returned, he would have forgotten all about her, and she was certain she would forget about him by then too.

After all, it was just sex.

ABOUT THE AUTHOR

Paranormal romance author Aria Chase combines her fascination with the occult and her undying love for happily ever after to create steamy shifter reads that are perfect for devouring in one night.

Connect with Aria online:

www.ariachase.com

ALSO BY ARIA CHASE

Emerald City Shifters

Bearly Breathing

Polar Bond

The Bear's Secret Baby

One Night With A Bear

Fighting For Her Bear

Bought By A Bear

Sundown Wolves

Temptation

Reparation

Distraction